LAUGHTER, MOON & C

Pavitra Menon

INDIA · SINGAPORE · MALAYSIA

Notion Press

Old No. 38, New No. 6
McNichols Road, Chetpet
Chennai - 600 031

First Published by Notion Press 2019
Copyright © Pavitra Menon 2019
All Rights Reserved.

ISBN 978-1-68466-383-5

FLINTSHIRE SIR Y FFLINT	
C29 0000 0846 854	
Askews & Holts	24-Mar-2020
AF	£11.99
FLIDEESIDE	

Dedication

Thanks, thanks to thee, my worthy friend,

For the lesson thou hast taught!

Thus at the flaming forge of life

Our fortunes must be wrought;

Thus on its sounding anvil shaped

Each burning deed and thought.

'The Village Blacksmith'
by
– Henry W. Longfellow

Not everyone can be king. For some, it is the scorching heat of furnaces, the incessant hammering and toil. To my dad, who believes that hard work never kills and to my mom, who stood steadfast and believed in her two daughters, I dedicate my first book.

Foreword

The sky is bright blue. The chirping of the birds is drowned by the sounds of industrious men and women hard at work at the banks of a River. She is their goddess, Saraswathi. Stories of her magnificence and her generosity pull the community together; fear of her wrath keep them on the straight and narrow. In the organised streets are a band of cheerful kids and their platoon of toys that hurtle down the roads with wild and merry abandon. There are no fortifications, just the flurry of open exchange between citizens and their guests from Mesopotamia; no garrisons, just peace-loving communities; no complex companies, just a thriving commerce of exquisite handicraft and necessary services; no elaborate architecture, just simple beauty in symmetry and handmade bricks; no indulgence, just the rationed enjoyment of nature's produce.

And with the click of a finger, it was all gone. Vanished.

4000 years later, in 1827, a deserter from the East India Company army observes strange mounds and an old citadel. Charles Masson doesn't know that the odd bumpy city is a veteran. His adventures are quickly followed by the work of Sir Alexander Cunningham in Harappa and Rai Bahadur Daya Ram Sahni and R.D. Banerjee at Mohenjo Daro. With every new excavation, one thing becomes clear: this is no humble settlement but a megalopolis.

The Indus Valley Civilisation is the largest of the four ancient urban civilisations. It could quite easily be the most magnificent or the most repugnant, the most awesome or the most awful. Say what you will and you could be correct because its truth is a mystery. Indus Valley seals and friezes, terracotta fragments and shards of toys languish in museums. Their true spirit suffocated by their inability to speak. To make matters worse, it is believed that a large number of relics were lost under the machinery of railway contractors that fulfilled the railway ambitions of the East India Company.

The story of the greatest civilisation remains locked within an undeciphered script. Why this lethargy in dispelling one of the greatest mysteries?

Until the early nineteenth century, the great civilisations of Mesopotamia and Egypt were deafeningly quiet too. But hidden amongst the numerous relics and artefacts were two stones that would shatter the silence: the Rosetta and the Behistun. The former authored by priests in praise of their Pharoah and the latter authored by Darius the Great, each contained three different scripts. Under the auspices of persistence and luck, the unknown and known script on these stones became the grooves; the single-mindedness of the French Scholar, Jean Francois Champollion, and the English Orientalist, Sir Henry Creswicke Rawlinson, became the needle and the Gramophone began to sing the haunting melodies of these two great civilisations. These tunes mesmerise to this day.

In the Department des Antiquités Orientales, Musee du Louvre, Paris is a cylinder.[1] It is a small barrel-shaped object with a small hole through the centre. It is engraved on the

---

[1]   Possehl, Gregory L. What in the World: Shu-ilishu's Cylinder Seal, Volume 48.2004

surface with various images. When rolled onto wet, malleable clay, it leaves an impression of a seated scholar holding court amongst a number of disciples. Shuilishu is rumoured to be a translator from the village of Akkad, a Mesopotamian village that hosted the Meluhhans. He lived in ca 2020 BC. What if his greatest work hasn't been found as yet? And what if, perhaps, that cosmic gramophone has one more record to play 2020 years this side of the Common Era?

And this is where fact ends and my story begins....

Contents

PART 1
1842–1857

1

Prologue

The Governor, Western Ghats 1842

'Can you hear me?'

He heard a scraping in response. It was reassuring. It was the only way to tell that within the mud sarcophagus lay a living breathing human being. The man had been pulled out of a burning factory. The Governor had wondered how that task had been undertaken. How do you pull a burning body? What do you grab that is not peeling, withering or falling off?

He looked at the clay invention in front of him. A tube was visible. It connected to the mouth of the patient within. He thought of the plight of the man inside. Organs had been badly damaged and the face completely burnt. The doctor had spoken of transplants ! It excited the Governor. Anything pioneering did.

He had wound up business in Hong Kong. A new chapter awaited in India. His plans were taking hold. The company directors in Calcutta had been more than agreeable. And then there was the pivotal shipment he had wanted to receive personally. It was what had led to this moment.

In the depths of the Western Ghats, inside a stone lodging guarded by sentries, a battle had ensued for the last ten days between two men. In the throes of deep agony, tossed through scorching nightmares and sleep denied, the former had battled within the walls of the mud sarcophagus. It had separated him thinly from the land of the dead. Whilst the latter, a man worshipped by his tribes people as god on earth, had flung himself into the battle. He had faced the challenge armed with herbs and barks, with chants and poultices. Whilst the patient wished for pain numbing sleep, the doctor had denied himself a single night's rest. After ten days of a raging fight, restorative sleep had come to both. The patient had been stabilised.

These were his best recruits; One a Captain in the Bombay presidency and the other a tribal doctor, they would help the Governor realise his vision for the Firm. He took pride in recruitment. Every employee was a prized sapling in his forest of ambition.

'Captain, you will make a full recovery.'

The scratching was tentative but it was there nonetheless. For a man that hadn't eaten in ten days, whose body now waited a new carapace, the patient was showing a defiance that made the Governor swell with pride but he didn't show it. The Governor looked at the doctor who was seated in front of the mud tomb packing more herbs into the clay.

'The chest has gone but it isn't your mistake.'

The scratching became vigorous. The doctor looked up in alarm. He checked the tube that connected to the mouth. It was intact. He turned to look at the Governor.

'I know you will not rest until you find them.'

The scratching stopped.

Amongst the cargo of hundred chests, the bronze chest had been the smallest. It had spent thousands of years buried in the sands of Mesopotamia. Local shepherds had spoken of the haunted circle, the sacred circle where none must visit lest they disturb the ghosts of the dead. But the Governor and his tomb raider friend knew that tombs were the gateways to invaluable opportunities. The chest had been found in an inconspicuous tomb, small and plain to escape attentions of the untrained but not his. It had contained a map; it was the reason why the Governor had moved his base of operations to India.

But that chest and map had been stolen under the watch of the Captain. Unable to withstand the guilt, the Captain had set fire to the armaments factory locking himself and forty of his infantry with him. What the Captain didn't know was that for the Governor, the theft was an intended outcome. It had been part of his plan all along.

Diversifying into a business with dependence on the past was not without its challenges. Witnesses were not forthcoming because they were mostly dead. Evidence lay scattered and hard to find. Precious nuggets that were passed down from generation to generation lay in the hands of the privileged. The Governor would find the shards of evidence, the legends and the old wives' tales. But he needed more. He had a theory about the map. He discussed the possibilities with intellectuals. He shared his hypothesis with colleagues, all the time laying a trap. He had made a copy of the map. Of course, he had. He was the Governor; he didn't take chances. The target had fallen for the bait. And now they would lead him to *It*.

'Your new lodgings have been arranged. Wait for my instructions.'

And find me the perpetrators. He thought the words. He didn't need to say them to the Captain.

2

Unlikely Incumbents, Unlikely Friends

Calicut, India 1852–1853

Chiri (Charlotte)

Calicut didn't care about first impressions. She didn't tidy up and her house was a mess. Her children wallowed in the mud, unchecked. Her dogs, cats, cows and pigs came and went as they pleased. Housekeeping was left to the mischievous winds, which swept more in than they swept out. Huts on the beach were just props; the household business of her people took place on the beach for everyone to see. I was pretty sure we had taken a wrong turn and docked in the wrong subcontinent.

I had heard stories of people who had returned to England from India, laden with gems, jewels and exquisite silks. They had conjured images of marble palaces and sparkling fountains and had spoken of exotic fruit, food and spices. Determined not to be outdone, I looked for gold and silver and found it in the scales of fish on butcher blocks, not jewels but jewel tones in the feathers of kingfishers, silks in the wings of butterflies and diamonds in the teardrops that glistened in the eyes of begging children.

Not far from the jetty, horses imported from Arabia jumped off arriving ships and galloped across the water to the beach with cheering spectators. Back then, I wanted to gallop too. But in the opposite direction and on the next ship back to England.

We arrived in India in 1852. Papa had accepted a position as a doctor to the Zamorin of Calicut. The Zamorin was like the Maharaja. I liked the sound of the word 'Zamorin'. It would be the Zamorin who would christen me 'Chiri', which meant laughter in Malayalam.

The decision to bring me to India had been difficult for my parents. The journey was dangerous and there was always the risk of catching something nasty. But Mama was dead set against sending me to boarding school in England.

We arrived in a country that had stunned our senses and in that state of mild concussion; we met N Kutty (Narayanan Kutty), our manager. His white *mundu* and cleanliness stood out in that melee of filth and disorganisation. N Kutty was a limited edition of the Calicut male, bereft of belly and ample moustache; although, a puny excuse for the latter gleamed, anointed in oil.

N Kutty rattled on excitedly about the house we would be staying in and how lucky we were to have it. He was the caretaker and had looked after the *Nalukettu- Maradu-Tharavadu* for twenty years. Most houses in Calicut had names built to lock the jaws of the English.

We were introduced to SM Street—the bustling centre of Calicut. Several rows of higgledy-piggledy buildings were stacked against one another. It was chaos upon chaos, people upon people and noise upon noise. I remember the shock I had when our *Judka* (horse cart) stopped abruptly in the middle of the street. Surely, our house was not in the middle of this mad merry-go-round!

Thankfully, the tall, white structure with its grand doors was only the gatehouse. I picked up the Malayalam word for gatehouse very quickly. *Padippura.* Probably because it sounded so much like *Parappu Vada,* a snack to which I had developed a dangerous addiction.

The house would eventually grow on me but it was the *Kulam* (bathing pond) that got my full attention. Enclosed on three sides by a huge moss covered wall, the entrance was dramatic, complete with a bronze studded door and a descent through steep, granite steps. It was like an exquisite painting: an emerald green sheet of glass surrounded by a ribbed granite frame. It took on different colours during the day and at night, it reflected the star-studded heavens. It also explained why Indians were so keen on bathing. Who wouldn't want to immerse themselves in its cool waters?

Apart from the *Kulam,* my other favourite haunt was the balcony, which was situated on the upper storey roof. It was also where I escaped to with my scrapbook, which I filled with illustrations: the *Kulam,* the evolution of moustaches and a temple elephant that paid us a visit the day we arrived.

It was afternoon. Mama and Papa were being ceremonially led along the line by N Kutty so they could be introduced to the house staff. There was a commotion by the gatehouse. I was perched on the balcony. The trunk appeared first, then came the pillar-like, podgy legs and the grey, boulder-like body. The poor mahout had a less dignified entrance. He spilt into the forecourt and was gasping for breath. She ambled through as if she were a member of the family and helped herself to the water kept in a brass bucket on the step. Mama and Papa, who were halfway through the imposed inspection, stumbled into the staff in shock. Janani, the revered temple elephant, was on state visit now.

Janani strolled along the line and stopped at intervals to inspect the armpits and heads of people with her bristly trunk. She rustled Mama's skirt and lifted it slightly. If Mama had been having a cardiac arrest, she didn't let on. I could see that the trunk had caressed Mama's bad foot. Janani then lifted her trunk, drew Mama and Papa close together and sprayed their heads with water. There was a gasp from the staff as they knelt before her. She repeated the same, this time showering everyone. And then Janani turned to look at me like she had known I was there all along. I thought I saw her smile.

Baskets of bananas, pineapples, coconuts and rice balls materialised from the air. News of Janani's impromptu visit had spread across the town and the industrious people of SM Street had rallied into action. The famous Calicut hospitality was being called upon and there was no effort spared. Janani was the mascot of the Thali temple. She was a celebrity.

She accepted everyone's offering. Baskets of fruit and grain disappeared under her trunk, descending into a bottomless pit while the mahout let out a string of protests.

Each of the residents of our new home indulged her. If I had thought our new home would be just ours, I was wrong. The Tharavadu was a colony of people and families. I thought they were our servants but that didn't seem right. At first, I didn't know who they were or what roles they performed. There was no evident order or dress code. Mothers, fathers and children were engaged in the running of the house, our house. I didn't remember ever knowing the children of our maids in England or what their lives were like outside of work.

Outsiders who had come to pay homage to the elephant were efficiently organised into groups by N Kutty and escorted to the front of the house, where they sat around the tamarind tree. He returned to the courtyard where he had a hurried discussion with Girija Edathy, who said something quickly to her deputy. Instantly, everyone disappeared only to reassemble with various contraptions. We were having a party. I left my observation point and sat on the platform that bordered the courtyard. The roles of each member of the household started to become clear.

Girija, the reassuringly plump cook, had commanded a production line. (To me, the mark of a good cook was in her good proportions). She led the manufacturing by cutting banana leaves. These were then smeared with rice paste. A beautiful girl churned out mountains of grated coconut. A man with a limp garnished the coated banana leaves with shredded coconut and jaggery. The parcels were dunked into large copper-lidded vessels that hissed with steam. A brother and sister duo fished the parcels out of the makeshift outdoor stove and arranged them on huge platters, which they distributed to waiting guests.

'I Soundarajan.' A voice interrupted the recital. I looked at the boy with his brown face, golden hair and blue eyes. '*Muthashi*,' he said, peering at my face. 'Very nice to mate you.'

He pushed a banana-leaf parcel into my hand. A harried woman appeared at my side. She apologetically mumbled a volley of words in Malayalam and led the boy away. The boy continued to gesture at me. I heard him say the word '*Muthashi*' again.

Mama took my palm and squeezed it. She took the banana-leaf parcel from my hand and started to peel it away, exposing the white cake inside. 'Here, I am told this is an *ada*. It is sweet. You will like it.'

'I've been thinking,' Mama said. She paused expectantly.

I was a bit wary of Mama's thinking episodes. They generally resulted in a new academic pursuit for me. 'Thinking of what?' I asked dubiously.

'What do you think of teaching?'

'Definitely not.'

'Not you Charlotte. Me. Me teaching.'

'You have no experience, Mama.'

'Yes of course grandmother.'

Mama turned to the boy who was still talking to his mother in half-baked English. Soundarajan was sitting on his mother's lap.

'What is *Muthashi*?' Mama asked the boy.

'Gramnuther,' the boy said with a smile.

'Grandmother?' Mama asked.

The boy nodded.

'Her?' Mama pointed to me, giggling. I frowned.

Janani didn't give me much chance to dwell on it for at that moment, she stood up to leave. An unseen force brought everyone to their feet in a show of reverence. She had presided gracefully over the party that had been thrown in her honour. The mahout brought her more water. Her handkerchief-like ears shook off flies. The bells on her feet made a tinkling sound. She stood still. I looked at her, my mind in a tangle. I wanted to offer her food like the others had but fear had got the better of me.

'Would you like to feed Janani?' Another boy had materialised. Evidently, he could read minds. He was tall and lean. I hadn't seen him until now. He offered the basket of bananas for me to hold. I refused.

He stroked Janani's trunk; her eyes glistened, her jaws puckered and a smile appeared at the corner of her mouth. She picked up the basket and shovelled the contents into her mouth. 'It's easy. Here take this.' He gave me a bigger basket and pressed it into my hand. He was persistent. I looked at the mark of ash on his forehead; tiny specks fell on his nose. I didn't listen to anything he said. My attention was focused on his dense eyebrows and the way small depressions appeared on his cheeks when he spoke.

When his attempts at verbal communication failed, he resorted to touch. He put his hand on my shoulder and urged me into the path of the elephant. I had transformed into a puppet in his hands. She accepted my hesitant offering as though she had been waiting for it all along. She dipped her trunk into the bucket and showered drops over me. I giggled.

I turned around to thank the boy but he had disappeared. Instead, I found the pot of grey ash that had been used to welcome the elephant. I dipped my fingers into the powder and spread it on my forehead. It cooled my forehead and disciplined the sweat that had been running, unhinged, down my forehead. My eyes captured a single fleck that had dropped from my forehead and then met the gaze of N Kutty, who looked at me with a peculiar expression. I rubbed the ash off with a jerk.

A torrential downpour concluded our first evening in Calicut. The rains couldn't wait to meet us. That is what N Kutty had said. Except, the rains hadn't come because of us. Nature was grieving. Janani had died that night. Lightning and thunder ripped through the town. The gutters overflowed. The filth of the streets was displaced temporarily by the bloody rain. The red rain had struck at the very moment Janani breathed her last.

A stone mound appeared on the floor of her enclosure at the Thali temple. It had been discovered the day after her death by her devoted mahout. It was as though the mound had pushed through the granite floor of the temple. It had the markings of ash and sandalwood as if it had been given a sacred send-off from the subterranean before arriving.

I did wonder if Mama's idea to teach was because the heat had gotten to her that first day. But when she embarked stolidly on her idea to bring English wisdom to Soundarajan and the rest of the native staff, she proved me wrong. As it panned out—and annoyingly, like all parent's ideas—it was for the best. For one, there was only so much lounging around in the *Kulam* and drawing I could fill my day with. And as much as I adored my mother's companion, Carly, and how she sufficiently widened my horizons with her discourses on love and men, I needed to be in the company of children.

We didn't speak the same language but breaking the ice did not need one. Radha, the quiet girl who had served the *adas* on that first day, had chosen to sit with me during the first lesson. We shared a bench. Aaji, Radha's adopted brother, sat on the ground. Soundarajan, pulled a chair and sat next to Mama, at the head of the room, and spent the entire class examining Mama's books and pamphlets.

Calicut began to grow on me. I became accustomed to the sight of children soiling the beaches and the commotion amidst the fishermen. But the sight of old men pulling their boats into the sea stung my eyes every single time. The chaotic SM Street began to make sense. It was a circus of hard-working people going about their lives, trying to earn a living.

A musty odour clung to Calicut. Her clothes were worn and dirty, her hands calloused and rough and her breath hot and sticky. But her arms were wide open. In the solidarity between animals and humans, she found peace. When her children slept, she tidied up and returned everything to their rightful place so, in their waking hours, her people found a paradise. The smelly fog had lifted, the brocade green sparkled and the emerald sea dazzled. Her wealth was in her poor people, who checked if others had eaten. Her people, in turn, expressed their gratitude to her in the lamps they lit at dusk. It turned her many meandering streets into garlands of luminescent pearls.

'Good night, my dear Janani,' he said as he crouched next to her. Her breathing was heavy. For a hundred years, she had been the principal, welcoming the new incumbents into the fold. She knew she didn't have long. With a last ounce of strength, she had fulfilled her duty that day. The Zamorin took the veshti from around his shoulders and beckoned for the oil to be brought. He dipped it in the oil and rubbed her trunk. 'You have worked tirelessly. And now, you must rest.'

Sarah

'Evil Lynn won, Papa.'

'Don't call her that, Sarah. She is your aunt.'

"Don't climb trees," she said. Now, I can't. "Don't run in the house." Now, I can't. "Don't laugh so loud." I don't feel like laughing anymore. She won.'

'You will get better.'

'He called me Saaru.'

'Who called you that?'

'The bald man. He was standing next to you. I remember the smell and the smoke.'

'Smoke?'

'He said it would make me better.'

'How can you remember him? You were unconscious!'
'I remember him, Papa. Who is he?'

'He is the man who told me the Tales, Sarah.'

'Shu's stories? Can you tell me a story, Papa.'

'Do you remember where we stopped?'

'There was a land, a long time ago. On two sides, it was surrounded by emerald green seas and on one side, by a sapphire blue ocean. The people were magnificent. They were clever and beautiful. Their *land was paradise. Not only because it had the greenest of trees, the liveliest of animals, the loveliest of flowers and the sparklingest of rivers but because they were all equal. They had a prison for evil aunts, mothers never died and fathers did not disappear for months together.'*

'Is that Shu's story or Sarah's story?'

'Continue the story, Papa.'

'Did I tell you about the monkey people who lived on this land?'

'Monkey people?'

'They lived in the trees and had many talents. They built bridges with stones. They were loyal and incredibly resourceful. And their leader was exceptionally strong. Once, a man had been fatally injured. The only cure was rumoured to be a plant that grew on a mountain. He searched up and down and far and wide. But he couldn't find it. Sounds like someone we know?'

'Papa, don't tease. I do find things eventually. What did he do next?'

'He scaled the mountain at an awesome speed and plucked a stem from every plant and a branch from every tree and brought them back.'

'Then?'

'They found the cure and were able to save the man. From then on, he became their hero. He was called the bearer of the mountain, one with lightning legs and hands.'

27

I was eleven when polio paid me a visit. It left me with a damaged leg and broken confidence. I was a hapless paper boat at the mercy of life's currents. I lived vicariously through the stories of Papa and Uncle's travels. Little did I know that fate had other plans and that I would push the frontiers of our two hundred acre estate in Wiltshire. Twenty five years hence, I was traversing the wake of the pioneers that had gone before. My destination, Calicut!

James's job offer—a personal surgeon and physician to the Maharaja of Calicut had caused ripples of chaos and excitement in our household. Before this, I hadn't known a place called Calicut even existed. James had reservations about taking Charlotte with us. It was I who insisted. Boarding school was not an option for my daughter.

I would miss home and my brother terribly. Grosvenor Hall had been Stanley's wedding present to us. Stanley also gave us a very generous allowance that more than covered the maintenance of the estate. He called it the dowry and would tease that it was a paltry award to James for taking me out of his care and responsibility.

Not one for current affairs, my country's accomplishments on land and sea had bypassed me. But on the deck of the East Indiaman, the buzz of the port was infectious. Clippers, steamers and sail ships paraded. Tradesmen and porters dashed around. Uniformed officers trooped in and out. The recent victories over Spain and France echoed in the confident stride of people and ships. Globe-trotting crates of Chinese tea, Indian chintz, North American hardwood, Canadian salted fish, Chinese silk and Jamaican sugar disembarked while bleak crates of my country's exports—wool, coal, copper, tin and yours truly—climbed aboard to travel to exotic places.

Carly, my friend and an unrelenting romantic, had packed her bags to India even before I could ask. She had an eventful journey full of seasickness, lovesickness and wardrobe emergencies. She was introduced to a dapper naval officer one evening. 'That one's a Bingley,' she had whispered with utter conviction when he was out of earshot. Carly's 'Bingley' had promised to take her around the ship's kitchen that day. She then spent the best part of the day trying to squeeze in and out of various gowns. Her mood was impaired by seasickness and it further irritated her that her endless bouts of vomiting had not affected her girth.

The sea had a reverse effect on James. He was like a child, excited by the sights and sounds. Each experience was a ratification of the knowledge he had gleaned through his voracious reading. He devoured history like Carly devoured penny dreadfuls and I devoured cake. Over dinner, while Carly flirted with the handsome, decorated officers and I marvelled at the spread, James remarked that there had been no uniforms and no system of ranking in the navy until a hundred years ago. He spoke of the unappetising weevil-infested sea biscuits and salted beef stew that sailors would eat before, until someone (the name escapes me) found ways to source fresh food on ships, enabling crews to be stationed for long periods of time without starvation and disease. This was my cerebral James.

But James had formed close friendships with the senior officers of the East India Company and spent hours drinking and gambling with people who were not his type. The James I married didn't drink and despised gambling yet on the ship, rum and rummy had become his best friends. The changes in his behaviour were perplexing and he dismissed my questions. There was a part of James's world that was being locked away. I wasn't welcome there and it hurt.

'*A Seer had seen the future. It would all come to an end. Their beautiful homeland would be destroyed.*'

'*What is a Seer?*'

'*A sage.*'

'*Then what happened, Papa?*'

'*Some fled across the seas and settled in the lands of Mesopotamia.*'

'*What about the others? The others remained?*'

'*Yes, the others stayed. Their hopes rested on the shoulders of the Seer who had guided them through many turbulences before. The Seer spent fourteen years in penance to find a solution. One day, he emerged from the forests and announced that Meluhha would live if they followed his plan.*'

'*What was his plan?*'

'*It was a great undertaking. The giant structures they had built were dismantled. The exquisite art they had commissioned in ceramics, metalwork and lapidary were removed from walls and sorted and organised into packages. Their knowledge of flora and fauna were transcribed into parchment and stored in neat bundles. Observations on astronomy, astrology and medicine and their literature and social discourses were inscribed onto stone panels and–*'

'*Packing! Is this all he could come up with after years of penance?*'

W hen the shores of Calicut loomed before us, it didn't excite me. Six months of anticipation had bubbled over and left a pool of tepid water.

James had grown more distant. My mind tossed between the past and the present. A countless indiscernible thoughts dispersed from and merged with my brace. It was always the brace. The wooden callipers had been James's engagement gift; it began our courtship. Now, it pricked and hurt.

The enchantment of the house did not last. Minutes after the temple elephant's visit, James declared that he had to go and would possibly not return for a few days. No other explanation was given. It crept on us like a thick, silent fog. A sinking feeling gnawed at my insides like water lashing against paper.

It was in that situation that I made a friend in the *Tharavadu*—Krishnan Kutty, a paper boat just like me. He stretched his arm out, offering a cloth which confused me. 'For wiping,' he said, gesturing to the wet patch on my shoulders and my head. I'd forgotten how the elephant had showered James and me only moments earlier.

'The water will bless you. Janani is the messenger of the Mother Goddess.'

I was sceptical. The holy water had come from a brass bucket filled with water from the well.

K Kutty couldn't climb coconut trees like most of the men in the Tharavadu. So he stood at the bottom of the tree to provide guidance on which coconuts to pluck, which weren't ripe yet, which were precarious and which, if not removed, would fall and hurt somebody. He would help Girija, our cook, by selecting the beans, yam and pumpkins from the vegetable patch outside. In the mornings, he would wait outside my room with a cup of coconut water to drink and a bronze bucket of water to wash my face.

'A bayonet pierced my leg,' he said one day, pointing to his right leg and explaining the unnatural bend. There were other injuries too. Some were visible and others were hidden behind his sad eyes. He didn't look at my leg and neither did he ask.

But I felt obliged to share what I had found difficult to talk about with anyone else.

'Polio,' I said softly, afraid that uttering the word would bring it back.

There was empathy on Krishnan Kutty's face. 'Does it hurt you? The humidity can make it terrible.' he said, pointing to my specially adapted brace. I nodded.

'Rub coconut oil on your leg every day before you put on the brace. It will stop hurting you. I will bring you some oil. It helps everyone in the *Kutumbam*. My son, Aaji, massages it onto my leg sometimes. My Radha drinks it so that she will become fat like your Charlotte. It helps Narayanan Kutty with his motion.'

'Motion?' I asked, confused.

'Loosens bowels,' he said and then kept quiet. We looked at each other and began to laugh. The two Kuttys were poles apart: Narayanan Kutty, the polished manager, and Krishnan Kutty, a man with no specific role yet indispensable to the house.

Recovering from his laughter, he said, 'In this house, we know each other's secrets, your Ladyship.'

I looked at him. His gaze shifted momentarily from my eyes to somewhere behind my head.

'I have cleared the plate room, Ladyship.'

He pointed to the 'plate' room. Food prepared in the kitchen was brought there to be ladled into special crockery. The staff ate on banana leaves. The plates had been brought in just for us. Krishnan Kutty had made it his responsibility to take care of the expensive China that had been sent specially by the Zamorin.

'Cleared the room? I don't understand, Kutty.'

'It will be a good room for teaching. That boy Soundarajan is very keen but also very hopeless in English. If you teach, my Radha and my Aaji will join too. It will help Emily too.' he said, smiling at Charlotte, who had just walked in through the door. She was returning from her four hundredth visit to the *Kulam*. It had taken a hold on her.

'Who?' I asked Krishnan Kutty.

'Charlotte,' he said, pointing at her. It was an innocent but strange mistake. He couldn't have possibly known that Emily was Charlotte's middle name, after James' mother?

--->>><<---

It was the middle of the night. Not a soul stirred. Smoke emerged from a bronze pot. The porcelain cohabitants of the plate room watched as the vapours wafted like a bride. She carried with her a medicinal bouquet as she glided across and made her way to the room. She crept up to the nose of the woman who slept. Over two decades ago, the vapours had given Sarah strength and helped her recover from polio. This time, it had another mission: To make her remember the stories and make her ready to lead.

--->>><<---

Chandran

On the first and third Thursday of every month, I made my way to the beach before sunrise and walked to where it ended in a wall of rocks. Here, a cliff jutted out into the sea like a gigantic saw. I swam to the cove on the other side. I had chosen this location deliberately. The shallow waters were dotted with hazardous rocks that kept the fishing boats away, leaving it secluded and ideal for our meetings.

In the silence, I could hear my thoughts. The swim had jostled them around; they moved haphazardly like dust particles in a sunbeam. I lay on the small stretch of beach. My thoughts were regulated now, no longer bumping into each other like overenthusiastic devotees in a shrine. One thought surfaced again and again. Would Chacko make it this time? He had missed the previous meeting.

I remembered Kutty Ettan's words from our recent conversation. 'Everyone is being watched,' he had said a few weeks ago. 'Chacko needs to be more careful.'

Chacko was a daredevil.

It was a year ago, during Singaravelli's first performance in Calicut.

'Chacko, we didn't think you would come?' I asked. 'I am here now,' he said.

'Why so angry, Chacko? Kutty Ettan gave you a dose?' Aaji asked.

Chacko grumbled. Kutty Ettan's so-called dose was legendary.

'Chacko, you could have been caught,' I said.

'I am careful. Kutty Ettan knows that. And I got the job done.'

'But you went off script.'

'I left them a message. That is all.'

'More like redecorated the office building 'Aaji volunteered.

Chacko gave him a dirty look.

'The obituaries had to be written. Fifty-one farmers killed themselves because of the Company's cotton policy. I scribed fifty one names on the walls of their building so they wouldn't forget.'

Aaji and I didn't say anything. We understood his anger.

'It makes me angry that they get away with it.' He stopped abruptly and lifted his head to hear the music.

Singaravelli was on her Aalap. Her song was captivating. Her chorus had reached a crescendo. The piece culminated in the solo recital of the percussionist on his mridangam. 'Tha di keetha, tha di keetha thaka dhimi thom.' We had spontaneously joined during the chorus.

Chacko relaxed. He was his old self again. Our music lessons together were firmly planted in our memories.

'Have you been inside the steam loco, Chacko?' Aaji asked sensing that his anger had abated.

'Yes. Saw it in Rajahmundry. The Zamorin was there too. He rode the inspection coach with the Governor General.' Chacko replied, a glint in his eyes. I knew that look.

'You did not?' I asked incredulously.

'I did. I rode on top of them. Sat on top of the Governor General's head and he had not a clue. Swear on my mother. It was adipoli!'

Adipoli. Only he would dare to ride on top of a coach bearing the most senior British official and his escorts.

'They use the loco to carry stones for the dam construction. It is so noisy. At first, it felt like the land was on fire. Smoke was everywhere. Even the Godavari felt intimidated.' Chacko said.

'In a year or two, it will carry people. Kutty Ettan says so.' I replied.

It had happened within a year. The first passenger train had made its way between Bombay and Thane. Stations sprung up in remote villages; sometimes a pukka building and sometimes, a Banyan tree. Station masters, porters, firemen and engine drivers became a close-knit fraternity. Chacko had travelled brazenly without a ticket on all his journeys.

Chacko was our best operative. He had run between Cananore and Calicut in one night to deliver an important message. He was an expert at stalking people and dodging pursuers. But his true passion was for tailoring. He hoped to return to his father's business once this was over. Chacko had shown us the first lady's blouse he had stitched. He even modelled it for us, stuffing a mango in each cup to show the tailored fit. We had all taken turns to model the blouse, with mangoes jiggling on our chests.

It was Kutty Ettan who had enlisted us in the Cause. Some of us had run-ins with the law—some more than others. For instance, Chacko had been a regular guest at the central jail until the Cause found us. It tested our tenacity and our threshold. It taught us to master our anger and control our wrath.

Offloading and displacing their precious cargo, and disrupting the rail service by herding several water buffaloes onto a railway track released some accumulated anger against Company rule. Our meddling caused inconveniences and annoyance. But blood was never spilt—not by us. The Cause made us disciplined. It was rigorous and intensive.

And then Charlotte arrived. Like a train, she had steamrolled into my life without warning and turned it upside down. I remembered the run-up to the doctor and his family's arrival. It had taken days of continuous toil to prepare the house for its new guests. The Kulam had been spruced, the forests behind had been pruned, the wood and brass polished, the oxide flooring scrubbed and the cupboards, pillars and roofs were combed for wasp and snake nests. The Zamorin himself had visited to approve the results of the massive undertaking. There was no question that these were important guests.

The doctor was affable and his wife was considerate. But his daughter had inflicted invisible wounds. I went about my chores that day, rendered completely useless by her. Aaji, my best friend, followed in my wake, redoing what I had done and doing what I hadn't.

The sorceress had claimed my balcony on the very day of her arrival. It was where I generally conducted reconnaissance, monitored Kutty Ettan's moves and kept well-hidden so he wouldn't give me any more chores. I had been forced to resort to a less comfortable observation point—on top of a coconut tree. But Radha had found me that day. She wanted me to help Charlotte feed Janani, the temple mascot. Radha had said it was what Janani wanted. How she knew what was going on in an elephant's head was mystifying!

'Would you like to feed the elephant?' Seven simple words! But looking into Charlotte's eyes, saying those words and trying not to blush like a complete idiot had taken every ounce of will power and more. Her eyes were captivating, bright with curiosity and were framed and enhanced by dark lashes. Her face was fresh and translucent, in open defiance of the heat. The graze of her hand on mine sent a current through my body. No sooner had I helped her feed the elephant (as Radha had requested) I disappeared.

Bobbing up and down on the waves I saw a head. 'Chacko!' He is here. I rushed to the edge of the beach. Chacko was an excellent swimmer. Actually his long lists of feats were quite annoying. But one could never be jealous of Chacko. I waited as the head approached. I looked desperately for thrashing limbs. The head washed ashore. It was a terracotta pot with weeds. I laughed to myself. Hothead was one name for him. Pothead would be a good name too. It was Chacko who had come up with the names 'Boiling Mary' and 'Bull Frog' for the first foreign guests at the Tharavadu. Under Mary's reign, water was perpetually boiled and the floors and everything else barring us were incessantly scrubbed. Slimy and swollen Mr. Thompson had a convenient working arrangement. He spent days in discussions with a handful of people who frequented the house. His eyes followed Damayanthi everywhere. I didn't trust him and was relieved when the Thompsons left. We were sure Madhavan Nair had something to do with their swift exit. He had arrived as the house guard only a day before. It was a job that wasn't fit for a man of his mettle but Nair wasn't troubled by title.

Madhavan Nair was our undercover Kalaripayattu teacher. Whilst the Cause tested our nerves, the regime of Kalaripayattu steadied them. It was the one thing that kept our heads when many around were losing theirs. Aaji and I would disappear into a banana plantation every morning. Scooped out of the middle of the plantation was a square clearing or the *Kalari*. We practiced the martial art in secret because it had been outlawed by the Company since the time of Pazhassi Raja.

Although my father left when I was six years old, in the Tharavadu I acquired two father figures: Madhavan Nair a role model and Kutty Ettan, guardian and bonafide dictator. Kutty Ettan brought my mother and me to this house. I acquired a big family. Girija became my grandmother, Damayanthi and Subhadra my older sisters, Aaji was my best friend. Radha and Soundarajan were my little siblings. But Sound, Aaji and I had one thing in common. We were refugees.

Soundarajan had golden hair and blue eyes. 'Mixed blood' was how the British scorned him. Our people treated him far worse. His biological father, a British officer with the Chittoor regiment, had thrown his mother out when he found that she was carrying his child. Kutty Ettan had brought Subhadra to the Tharavadu with her unborn baby. In spite of a tenuous beginning, Soundarajan arrived in the world as a growing bundle of liveliness and cheek.

Aaji was my buddy. He was a devout Muslim and he could recite the Devi's prayers better than the priests he grew up with. His parents had been killed in a Mopilla and Namboothiri skirmish some years ago. He was brought up by the priests at the temple. It was on Radha's insistence that he was brought to the Tharavadu. She had adopted him as her brother and in doing so her parents found a son they could lean on.

It had been four hours. Still no sign of Chacko. I imagined our usual greeting. He would enquire '*Endha Vishesham*?' and in my two word response I would shrug my shoulders and purse my lips. '*Onnu Iliya*, nothing.' He would know immediately. From the stupid tell-tale smile on my face and my eyes that would refuse to meet his, he would know that my heart had done a number. I would surrender and admit that I have never felt this way and he would laugh his raucous laugh.

Charlotte was a soundtrack that invigorated me. She didn't have to look at me. She didn't have to speak to me. But she came with me wherever I went. When carrying out my weekly harvest of coconuts, she was the lively percussion I paced my climb to. When I scrubbed the granite steps of the Kulam, we sang a duet. And when I bathed the elders who had taken refuge at the temple, she was an enchanting melody. I imagined her watching me all the time. For that reason, I tried to become the best version of me. I would say this to Chacko and he would tell me that I had lost my mind. I had, in a manner of speaking.

The tide had set in. I couldn't wait any longer. If I didn't hurry the currents would make the swim back to shore difficult. Chacko had missed the rendezvous again. I felt emptiness in the pit of my stomach. Chacko was supposed to contact the Captain and confirm the arrival of the ship. Could Chacko have been caught? The cargo was crucial. It was our responsibility to receive it. Without Chacko, there was no way of knowing when and where the ships would arrive. My team was relying on me to dispatch the information. But it was information I didn't have.

'Raghu, one sugarcane juice please.'

Chacko sat in his usual place—a bench overlooking the exuberant Godavari. Watching her had a hypnotic effect. He remembered what *Muthashi* had said.

'The holy rivers are the offspring of Devi, the Earth Goddess.'

Muthashi had said a change was coming. The rivers couldn't hide their excitement. They had waited for hundreds of years.

'Jatayu has come. Once the victim of a demon and extinct for thousands of years, he has now returned stronger. And with every returning species, She comes closer.' She had said.

Muthashi was their beloved queen and honorary grandmother. She was a patron of the temple dedicated to the Goddess, the only white woman to hold the honour.

'Your sugarcane juice.' The voice broke him from his stupor.

'Where is Raghu?' Chacko asked. Raghu was Chacko's friend. At seventy-five, he was the most sprightly sugarcane juice vendor Chacko had ever seen.

'Raghu is unwell. I am his friend friend.' The man's voice cut through. Chacko took the glass and sipped the juice. A sixth sense made him look into the man's eyes. The grey pupils stared back like cold balls of granite.

Chacko's hands shook. The glass fell from his hands. The light faded at a distance. There was a piercing pain in his heart with the realisation that Raghu was not unwell. He was dead. Chacko would be too. He didn't mind dying. But Raghu! The world needed people like Raghu—gentle souls who wouldn't harm a fly but whose good deeds made the earth rotate on its axis.

He remembered Kutty Ettan's words. "The enemy is faceless."

The face of the assassin didn't seem human. It was like painted leather stretched on a skull. He was joined by another man, whose face was menacing.

Chacko's veins became turgid with the toxin and protruded through his skin.

In his stupor, he saw a familiar face. What was she doing here? Her bronze skin shone in the dusk. She didn't say anything, as was her nature. Her eyes glistened with the blue, black and grey luminescent network of a butterfly's wings in her pupils. She took Chacko's hand in hers and waited with him.

—➤➤◄◄—

Colin

It was not my finest moment. I had embarked on a ten thousand mile journey to arrive at a godforsaken place for a job that was not guaranteed on paper. Still, I had done stupider things before and had been in worse scrapes.

I knew two things: One, India held promise; two, the Anglicists and the Utilitarians had changed the education policy and created openings for young graduates like me in Indian schools and colleges.

Not too long ago, I had made a voyage, albeit smaller, to change my destiny. My destination then had been Liverpool. I had adopted England as my new home and the country's heroes as my role models. I chose to appreciate their pioneering spirit and learn from their pluck and courage. I could have hated the country and its oppressive people. But I chose not to.

In my opinion, there were two embodiments of British zeal: the Navy and the East India Company. The sea wasn't good for my complexion. It had been green (with sickness) the entire voyage. So I would have been useless to the former.

The earthly nabobs of the East India Company, on the other hand, were an option that appealed entirely to my constitution. It was what brought me to Calicut, India.

The three national treasures were my role models: Robert Clive, James Cook and Horatio Nelson. Clive had been a dog's body before he became an overnight mogul. I worked out that if I got a foot through the door of the East India Company, an improvement in status and wealth wouldn't be far behind.

As the port of my new life drew near, I imagined myself in Cook's shoes, standing on the deck of the 'Endeavour', savouring the discovery of Botany Bay. The reality wasn't as romantic. I forged my way—as I knew Nelson would—through the swarming beaches of Calicut and into my new life, with five shillings and my faithful umbrella as my only defence.

The bravado was short-lived. The lack of appointment to a formal job worried me. An acquaintance on the ship had told me about Lady Sarah Carringham's recent arrival in Calicut. She was the sister of one of the wealthiest and most influential peers in England. If I were to become indispensable to Lady Sarah, the East India Company would welcome me with open arms.

I wasn't altogether destitute and didn't have to run into Lady Carringham's arms as soon as I docked. Through my patron in Hertfordshire (I had worked as a footman for a wealthy Baron), I had been introduced to a lieutenant, who had invited me to stay a month at his magnificent guest house in Calicut.

It was at his house that I made the fortunate acquaintance with N. Kutty. I liked him immediately. For one, he didn't barricade himself behind an unwieldy name. (Malayali natives were very cunning. Their intimidating names were only for our benefit.) But Kutty was a man of 'Sahibs and Salaams', full of respect and admiration for the British. He had also masterfully managed the lodging for me in Lady Carringham's household!

The *Maradu Tharavadu* was a stately home owned by the Zamorin. It was enveloped by coconut trees. More prolific than the coconut was the range of wildlife: cockroaches the size of rats, rats the size of dogs, lizards ready to drop into your lap or on your head, multicoloured frogs and a variety of beetles and multi- headed snakes. My sabre'esque umbrella accompanied me everywhere—to the privy too. I did not, as a rule, open cupboards after sunset.

Evenings I spent at the Cosmopolitan Club. Membership of the Club was exclusive and open only to British officials. The Club was a temple to Britain. It provided patrons with a taste of the organised world they had left. It served only British food and ale. Cocktails were named in honour of the East Indian Company's military achievements: *Plassey Plunder, Tipu's Turmoil, Maratha Mayhem* and *Pickled Pazhassi*.

The drinks' menu boasted of a century of conquests. At the Battle of Plassey, the 'humble' merchant became the ruler. If Plassey were the aperitif, a meal was made of the Marathas. The Company's belly soon advanced from the taxation of Delhi, Agra, Bundelkhand, Broach, parts of Gujarat, Cuttack and Bombay. *Tipu's Turmoil* satiated their French obsession. Four wars were waged against the Mysore king, Tipu Sultan, who was an ally of the French. Pickled Pazhassi—a heady cocktail of absinthe and tamarind juice—was not very unlike the firebrand Pazhassi. The Prince regent of Kottayam had waged a guerilla war with the British over ten years ago. It came to an end when he was killed.

But perhaps it was in Ireland where it all began, where the imperial appetite was whetted.

It would be remiss of me to allow one to assume that I had landed free boarding and lodging in the *Tharavadu* on account of my good looks and personality. I was to be a tutor to the children of the native staff—a job shared with her Ladyship. It was a job I intended to do conscientiously and to the best of my ability, unlike Carly, Lady Sarah's companion, who believed that knowledge could be absorbed by respiration. She would happily stand in for Lady Sarah, mixing the Iliad with the Odyssey just like how she was convinced that she had mastered the local cuisine by subjecting every one of Beeton's recipes to lashings of grated coconut.

Lady Sarah's familiarity with the natives surprised me. Her programme of education was unexpected. To her, it was a symbiosis. It was their folk tales and mythology that she sought in exchange for lessons in the English language. She was so different from many of the aristocratic ladies I had known. I often saw her making her own bed, doing her own hair and even selecting her clothes on her own. She had developed a close friendship with Krishnan Kutty—the other Kutty in the household.

Kutty in Malayalam meant child and so did '*Unni*' and '*Kuttan*'. With the possibility of almost every Malayali grown-up male being an *Unni*, a *Kuttan* or a *Kutty*—Calicut was host to the biggest misnomer convention (Carly called the two Kuttys Cutie and Cutie!).

Classes were held in the plate room (or 'plight room', according to Soundarajan, the little terror!). It was not my choice but it was a room with good cross ventilation. Calicut was excruciating. My Victorian attire wasn't made for a climate like this. But I wasn't going to sacrifice my appearance for the sake of comfort. The officers of the Company had commissioned extravagant palaces to reinforce their status as rulers. I did not have a permanent roof over my head (forget palace) so my dressing was my only fortification.

I took a class just before mid-day and Lady Sarah took an hour in the evening. Where the natives went before and after the classes was not my concern. However, I was very interested in where Charlotte had been. She had a different dress for breakfast, lunch and dinner. I suspected Carly's involvement— the teaching assistantship and gastronomy wasn't stretching her many talents.

The members of the Club called me C, Colin being too discombobulating I suppose! But that had given me an idea. I created nicknames for my students (only unlike members of the Club, I could cope with more than one syllable). Chandran was Moon, a direct translation. Charlotte would be christened Chiri by the Zamorin and as he had rights to that name I called her the English equivalent – Laughter. Soundarajan became Sound, although frankly Noise may have been better suited to him and Radha stayed as Radha. And so did Aaji, who wasn't really Aaji. Let me explain.

It had been my second lesson. A tall Indian youth entered the classroom asking for Shaaji. I insisted that I had no one by that name in my class and went on to reproach the man for the unwanted disturbance and inconvenience. Aaji stood up, his teeth bared in a smile. It turned out that Aaji had been Shaaji all along. He had a stammer and the 's' eluded him. But everyone continued to call him Aaji and so did I.

I decided to make Radha the class monitor. I instructed her to rap the knuckles of those who didn't comply with a baton. But my plan soon backfired. It wasn't Radha's fault. It was Sound. He was the chief offender. He was in love with Radha so he made more noise to get her attention.

'Sound, you are incorrigible,' I said to him, one class. 'Encourageable?' he said.

'No. Incorrigible,' I said. 'Vat?' he asked.

'Not vat, Sound. What. W-H-A-T.' I said. 'VH-AAR-T,' he said.

'WHH-A-T,' I said.

'PHWWVVVVAAARrrrT,' he said.

'Oh JESUS,' I shouted. He ran out of the class and came back some minutes later with the milkman.

'Who is this?' I asked.

'Jesus.'

In the next few days Sound brought Mary, Joseph, Christ to my class which put an end to my swearing once and for all.

I got to know the staff and didn't have much trouble with them. They kept to their own business which suited me well. N Kutty was a man of great resource. K. Kutty on the other hand was a reserved man who became Lady Carringham's assistant. And then there was Mr. Nair who only surfaced at nights. I met him one day when I had returned late from the Club. He guarded the house which to me seemed a bit excessive. It was not like we were royalty but if this was the Zamorin's wish who was I to question it. His full name was Madhavan Nair. Madhavan Nair's moustache and beard gave him an air of formidability. If he were to shave it off, I was certain I wouldn't recognise him. Not that I would dare to suggest that he needed to shave. I wouldn't dream of it. Not long ago, a mutiny had broken out in South India in the name of facial hair. To a Hindu, setting foot outside the borders of their country led to the contamination of the soul; contact with a lower caste mandated several ablutions; but the blessings of a scruffy ascetic with matted, mite infested hair was the path to Nirvana.

It was then that the penny dropped. My path to greatness had become clear. I would be the lantern bearer to the deprived inhabitants of the *Maradu Tharavadu*. Through their intellectual rehabilitation, I would become the cynosure of the Club and my peers at the East India Company.

In the corner of a cupboard, below a pair of breeches, a shoot had sprouted from the ground and penetrated through the floor. It had shown remarkable resilience–a sapling taking on the intimidating rosewood. Its curled- up, delicate leaves leant on russet wood and fondly kissed the jacket hung on the railing. It was a potato plant of a variety that was known in Ireland as the 'lumper'. It had seen days of misery and blight. Here, several thousand miles away, it sought sanctuary in a cupboard—not much different to the tutor who was here for a second chance.

The Dutch Factory, Calicut

He walked north of SM Street after having stopped at the Huzur Office. He had chosen to walk and feel the heat and beads of sweat on his brow, hear the endless chatter of pedestrians and smell the mangoes, guavas, jasmine and *thetchi* flowers. For years, these sights and sounds had been intangible—a past that had seemed so distant and foreign.

Today, when he washed his face in the cool waters of the Mananchira Tank and played with the boys in the *Maidan*, the memories didn't seem so far fetched. He hung around to make sure he wasn't being followed. He had dreamt of this day. Soon he reached the old Dutch factory. He was spellbound by the drastic changes around him. Without directions, he would have never found the cleverly concealed entrance.

'Enjoyed the walk?' The old man greeted him. The joy on their faces was evident. The two were from different generations but they hugged like long lost friends.

'I have waited long to see this. It is bewildering. It is almost complete!' the young man exclaimed joyfully.

'There is still plenty to do, another furlong to tunnel through.' The old man smiled at his companion's childlike excitement.

They surveyed the rocky interiors in silence. 'I have something to show you. Wait here.'

He made a clicking sound with his tongue and a shadow appeared from behind. In the overall darkness of the chamber, it was hard to tell what the young man saw or whether it was anything at all. The only sliver of light streamed through from a slit in the ground several feet above. There was a gentle thudding and from the darkness emerged a most incredible sight. The shadow was a walking mountain. Or at least, that was his initial thought. The form became clearer with every slow, deliberate step. Its eyes peered sheepishly through its eyelids and a smile appeared from the edges.

'Hercules,' he gasped with disbelief and amazement. He stretched his hands out and she lumbered slowly up to him. 'You kept her.'

'Did I have a choice?' the old man answered with mock exasperation.

'She has grown!' He stroked its shell, mustering the strength for what he was about to convey. She intuitively moved into the shadows, sensing that the meeting was not about her. 'I received a letter. It was from the Captain.' the young man said hesitantly.

'The Captain is alive. The Goddess looks over us.' the old man spoke, his eyes widened with a small flicker of hope.

But the next piece of news would be shattering. The young man took a deep breath. 'Chacko was murdered. Chanakyan was behind it. He had an accomplice. ' He dispensed the words as quickly as he could manage.

'Chanakyan,' the old man uttered the name softly.

'Is it the Firm?' the young man asked. But he already knew the answer.

'Yes, it is them.'

'But why kill Chacko?'

'Chacko isn't the only one.'

'There are others?'

'You remember Sugu?'

The young man nodded, recollecting the walks he had as a young boy on the strong shoulders of his favourite relative.

'Sugu was my eyes and ears in Sindh. He joined the Punjab Irregular Force—a name that irritated him immensely. "Irregular," he would say. "What kind of stupid name is that?"' The old man paused. 'He did that so he could keep an eye on Her.'

The young man waited as his companion strung together his words. *She* occupied his every waking hour... *She* would have to be relocated from her resting place. That monumental task had landed on his fragile shoulders. His memory wasn't sharp. Arthritis had eaten into his hands and legs. Hunched, he looked even smaller.

'I hadn't heard from Sugu in a while. It had happened before but then Chacko would materialise with a message. Sugu trusted Chacko with the sensitive dispatches.' The old man stopped abruptly as if he remembered something. He turned to his young companion. 'You said that Chanakyan had an accomplice?'

The young man was hoping his companion had forgotten that small but consequential detail. 'Matheson.'

'He is alive! It cannot be.'

'The Captain is certain.'

'It is the Governor. It is his doing. This means that they will be coming for us.'

'But there is nothing to link us. Chacko wouldn't have given us up.'

'Not Chacko. Not Sugu. But the Thompsons may have.'

His young companion tried to digest this latest setback. Last he had heard, the Thompsons had been dealt with. They had been forced to leave to Ceylon.

The old man continued. 'They were in Bombay a month ago. I didn't think much of it at the time. But if Matheson has been resurrected, he and Thompson would have certainly met.'

'And they would have spoken about Madhavan?'

'It is bound to have come up in conversation.'

'So he will have to go?'

'Yes.'

The challenges ahead looked insurmountable.

The young man allowed himself to be distracted by the several crates lined up on the side. The recent cargo had been unpacked. Its contents were dipped in soot to hide the intricate relief work. He walked up to a vast panel that had been laid out on the granite to dry. With its new coating, it almost merged into its surroundings. The old man joined him. They marvelled at the frieze. His young companion took the black sludge from the vat beside and attempted to conceal the face – it was the only part of the vast relic that had resisted the sludge lining. But the lapiz lazuli and the mother of pearl eyes peered through it defiantly, the sludge slid helplessly to the sides. The old man felt an energy surge through his body. He felt invigorated. The young man stood up at that very instance, as though an unexplained force had lifted him onto his feet.

'I will make arrangements to go to Calcutta,' the young man said. He had toyed with the idea several times. Here, a sudden stroke of clarity had made it an obvious next step. Calcutta was the headquarters of the Firm. It was their only chance of staying ahead. 'Do not worry about me. I will keep you updated.' He knew his words wouldn't console the old man. It did little to console his own fraught mind. He had wanted to be here by his side.

The old man started to reply when he was distracted by a rustling sound. After a pause, the old man whispered, 'You must. The team in Bombay will wait for your messages.'

He paused to clear his throat. 'The Company intends to go ahead with the railways in Sindh. We have to work quickly. If our experiment works it will cause chaos for them and buy us time.'

In truth, he didn't have much hope for the experiment. It was a crude plan cobbled together in a kitchen. If this didn't work, only the heavens could help. As if on cue, the clouds burst open and sheets of chopping rain replaced the golden curtains of the sun's rays. The men got up to leave.

The old man made the clicking sound. The mountain like shadow reappeared. She had been waiting patiently behind the wings. The old man patted her leathery back. 'Poor Hercules! She will have to put up with me until your return.'

'The markings on her shell are just like stars. She is beautiful.'

There was no question. The terrapin's arrival was remarkable. It was like she had been sent from the heavens. She had landed on the boy's lap under the tamarind tree. His uncles had loved the tamarind tree and spent many hours as boys lumbering up its branches. Sometimes, they would survey distant oceans from its leafy mast and other times, they would model advanced pulley systems from its roots.

The landslide had taken them away. It could have taken more lives but it didn't. The Universe had mercy. But she rationed it. His uncles had miscalculated the tunnels but how could they have known. Five hundred metres under the earth, everything looked the same. They had taken a wrong turn and the drilling's impact was immediate. The mud engulfed them in seconds.

The terrapin had timed her arrival on the day after the cremation.

'You know, you could be quite creative with the name, since you found her,' his mother said.

'Are you sure there is no one like her in the world? None at all?'

'She swam the rivers thousands of years ago. She may have been bigger then and perhaps had a longer tail too. But no, there isn't one like her anywhere in the world. So you get to name her. Finder's privilege!'

He wrote a name down in his distinctive style, taking extra care with the 'e' so it looked like a terrapin shell.

'Hercules!' His mother read the name now stencilled in an elaborate typeface. 'Strange name for a girl.' They laughed.

3

A Royal Lunch
and a Vermillion Protest

Calicut, India 1854

Charlotte

The monsoon arrived in Calicut. It was the month of *Karkidakam*. The stench of the sewers was overpowered by the heady perfume of rain chopping against red mud. Everything seemed washed, polished and ready for inspection. The rains in England didn't smell of anything. Neither did they bring transformation in the scale they did in India.

The south-west monsoons were crucial. They determined the sustenance of the people. With fewer tracts of land available for food crops, furrows had to be made and seeds sown in time for the rain. A tiny miscalculation could wreak havoc. I had heard that this *Karkidakam* had been particularly harsh but secure in the house, I was ignorant of the plight of the people outside our gates.

At dusk Damayanthi would flood the house with smoke from burning camphor. Its fumes made my eyes water. Soujanya and Girija lit the lamps for Goddess Sita in the *Tharavadu* temple. They recited poems from the Ramayana every evening. Krishnan Kutty explained that it was customary to recite it during *Karkidakam*.

It was on one of these evenings that Karunakaran brought a message from the Zamorin. The Zamorin had invited us to join him for Onam lunch. Lunch at the Maharaja's was a big deal. Or at least, I thought so. But there was no great celebration or excitement. Perhaps the household had sensed a tragedy was around the corner.

The monsoon's deathly talons made Madhavan Nair its victim. Narayanan Kutty had found his body floating in the *Kulam* covered in blisters. The body and the water from the *Kulam* had been examined in Papa's clinic. It had cast a sinister light over the *Kulam*. No one ventured into it after that incident. Even the pillared corridor that connected it to the kitchen was forsaken.

A few days had gone by. I was overcome with a desire to visit the *Kulam*. I wasn't alone. Damayanthi was sitting on the steps, her legs dangling in the water. As I watched the waves lap against her legs, I imagined blisters develop on her bronze skin. She gestured for me to come close. In her arms, she nestled a shiny, brown egg. She didn't say anything and pointed to the rafters, where I caught a glimpse of a nest.

Perhaps the egg had fallen. She turned the egg again and again in her hand, as though she were toasting it over an invisible flame. I saw a crack this time. I wasn't sure if I had seen it before. The cracks became deeper and multiplied in number. While I almost fell off the step with excitement, Damayanthi was calm, as though eggs hatched in her hands all the time. A beak appeared, along with two eyes that looked like beady peppercorns.

'Jatayu,' she whispered as she kissed the downy fledgling on its head.

'Where is its mother?' I asked.

'Me,' she said and smiled.

Jatayu was also the name of the majestic vulture that had fought valiantly against the ten-headed demon, Ravan. His wings had been sliced when he had tried to save Sita from the demon's clutches. It was an extract from the *Ramayan*. There was no escaping the epic during the monsoon. Verses of the poem reverberated everywhere.

As the royal luncheon approached, Carly compensated for the lack of gaiety with her feverish preparation. She had elicited Sound and Aaji to find raw materials for her ensemble and mine. Mama had excused herself from Carly's ambitious project. The trio, Carly, Aaji and Sound, spent two whole days scanning the markets for bright pink silk.

The day arrived. I finally saw what lay behind the majestic *Padippura*. A red and brown tiled path led the eye to the main palace. It was a larger and grander version of our *Tharavadu*. On the right, I caught a glimpse of the courtyard of the *Kamala Maaliga*. It was a sprawling two-storey pavilion used for weekly music performances. We caught a glimpse of the enticing courtyard with its many granite pillars through the exquisite doors of the *Maaliga*.

Three big men greeted us. They looked pristine in their white tunics and beige *mundus*. An unassuming old man sat on an easy chair behind them near the *Charupadi*. My eyes darted around quickly, looking for signs of the king. I was startled when Narayanan Kutty, Damayanthi and Soujanya fell at the feet of the frail old man. One of the well-built men bowed to Mama. He led her to the Zamorin. He beckoned me to his side. He put his hand on my shoulder and led me inside the palace.

The Zamorin wore earrings, two conservative diamond studs and a ring with a large coral. Apart from this, there was nothing that gave any indication of royalty. He was dressed similarly to the others, in shades of white and off-white. We were embarrassingly overdressed, like elaborate puddings but Carly didn't seem the least bit affected by it.

I was overwhelmed as I accompanied the Zamorin into the bright interiors of his abode. I was unaware of Sound's presence beside me. I only realised it when I heard his words. 'It's a horror to see you, Your Eminence,' he said, sputtering with excitement. The Zamorin reciprocated with a simple, 'No, the horror is mine, Sundar.'

Inside the palace, overhanging eaves framed a panelled ceiling, each carved with a different pattern. The floors had tiles that were decorated with geometric patterns. They had been polished for the occasion. Teak pillars supported the eaves and surrounded the four courtyards. One of them had been designated for the luncheon and was already occupied by other guests.

A large tiered lamp occupied the centre of the courtyard, its long arms carrying glistening pools of oil and illuminated wicks. To the side were a group of musicians, who tuned their assortment of drums and stringed instruments. The details of the quadrennial temple festival were being planned. As the chief trustee of the temple, the Zamorin had organised nine *Ulsavams* (festivals). The next festival would be special and grand, commemorating the tenth anniversary of this tradition.

Observing my flitting eyes, the Zamorin encouraged me to explore the premises. A door beckoned and I opened it. Nothing could have prepared me for the sight that greeted me. Beyond the door lay ruins, a shell of a building. It was roofless, with collapsed walls and the foundation peeked through the clumps of shrubs and weeds. It was surreal.

Narayanan Kutty, who followed me, explained that the Zamorin had intentionally kept that part of the palace as it was. It was a reminder of the destruction caused by the Portuguese forces in the early 16th century, under Admiral Marshall Coutinho. The palace had been rebuilt around it. In the centre was a bronze bust of Kunjali Marakkar II, the chief admiral of the Zamorin's fleet. He was revered for his valiant stand against the Portuguese forces. The Kunjali Marakkars were Muslims who had offered their wealth and ships to the Zamorin in his fight against the Portuguese.

Girija explained the relevance of the day. Onam marked the end of *Karkidakam*. It was a harvest festival where the people prepared festive banquets and invited friends and family to celebrate months of hard labour.

Girija vanished into the palace kitchen to help with the preparation and I found myself in the company of the Zamorin in the grounds outside.

The Zamorin asked me if I would like to help with the *Pookalam*. I nodded affirmatively but didn't have the foggiest notion of what he was talking about. He indicated to a basket of flowers, each overflowing with colour. Some contained petals and others had whole flowers. Karunakaran, the Zamorin's messenger who had brought our invitation, quickly laid out a series of dots on the ground with rice powder. Then with the same dexterity, he joined the dots to reveal a geometric pattern, containing lotuses, parrots and diamonds that repeated around an octagon.

At this point, Radha started to fill in the diamonds with the yellow petals of the chrysanthemum. Taking cue from Radha,

Mama joined in, filling the parrots with marigolds while I stared, frozen in my place. But when Chandran gave me a handful of button roses, the stupor dissolved. Mama looked up from her work and gave me a knowing smile. I could feel the colour rising in my cheeks.

In the days that followed, I preferred to recollect an embellished version of events. The *pookalam* had extended for miles. The superfluous others had disappeared and Chandran and I were alone engrossed in filling in the parrots and lotuses with an inexhaustible supply of sweet-smelling roses. There was melodious music in the background and a gentle breeze. In reality there were far too many unnecessary people involved in the *Pookalam* and it was hastily concluded because it was time for lunch.

Lunch was to be served on plantain leaves arranged in rows on the floor. Everyone sat on the ground while Sethuraman, the Zamorin's personal guard, escorted Mama and me to sit on either side of the Zamorin. There was a low chair and stool which I presumed the Zamorin would use. But I was stunned when he gestured for Mama to use the chair. He had known that Mama would not be able to sit on the floor because of her polio. I found his concern touching.

Imprisoned in my whalebone corset, I wished for a chair and table myself. I cursed Carly's tailoring a few times. In my mind, I tried to figure out the best and quickest way to sit cross-legged. After many embarrassing attempts, I sat with my petticoats caught between my legs and my feet twisted beneath me. I tried not to think of how I would get out of this position with my dignity still intact. I was uncomfortable and my legs began to cramp. But I focused my attention on the Zamorin.

Before the meal, the group chanted, 'Ambitame, Naditame, Devitame.' I joined in and the Zamorin nodded approvingly. I had picked it up from Girija, who always sang it while she served us our meals at the *Maradu* house. Girija had said it was a salute to Saraswathi, the mother, the goddess and the river. Looking around, I recognised the images of the Goddess carved on the pillars and the tiles of the ceiling.

I expected the eating to begin. My stomach was now howling with hunger. The room felt dense with expectant silence. All at once several shadows fell into the room through the windows. A loud chattering accompanied the drumming on the roof tiles like the pitter patter of hailstones. It was frightening. Sound ran to the window and put his hand out. A hairy paw stroked it.

'Monkey people,' he squealed.

I heard a gasp from Mama. She turned pale. A large number of black-faced monkeys descended into the courtyard. A large tray filled with laddoos and marigold flowers had been left in the centre. I knew all about the wicked laddoo—a million succulent morsels packed into a delicious sphere, dotted with raisins and cashew nuts. Radha and I had helped Girija make hundreds of them for the temple only a few days ago. A considerable amount had ended up in my stomach.

The monkeys gathered around the tray and I half expected a battle over the confections. But there wasn't. They helped themselves to only one laddoo and a marigold, except for a militant young monkey who helped himself to more than the evident quota. He, it seemed, had not been to the monkey school of restraint and discipline.

In minutes, the monkeys disappeared. I watched the guests. Everyone was moved by the spectacle but none were stunned like Mama and me. I turned to the Zamorin, who broke the silence by crushing his *papadam*. He looked at me and saw the question mark stretched over my face.

'Chiri,' he said, looking at me. There and then I was christened with my new name, with no ceremony but in surroundings sufficiently auspicious. 'Before you, before me and before this palace, was a forest. It was home to the monkeys, birds, trees and insects. They let us live here. We are because of them. So when we give thanks to the Earth Goddess for her bounty, we cannot forget them.'

A procession bearing trays of sweet and cauldrons of savoury heralded the much-awaited lunch. We were treated to an endless array of vegetarian dishes. The Zamorin picked at the small portion of rice and *papadam* on his leaf. By the Indian measure of wellbeing, the Zamorin was in a terrible way. He was thin, small and shrivelled—very far from a Malayali's definition of health and prosperity.

But his eyes were sharp, he was generous with his smiles and, though he spoke little, his utterances were meaningful. He addressed every guest by name, enquiring after their family members. Mama looked extremely conscious in her elevated position in the dining room as well as of her proximity to the King of Calicut. Turning to Mama, the Zamorin said gently, 'Do you like Calicut, Lady Sarah?'

'It is most agreeable,' Mama said hurriedly, hoping she wouldn't have to say anything more to his Highness.

'I hear you are teaching the staff. They speak highly of you.'

Mama turned to Mr. C who, squeezed between two stocky farmers, was a picture of unhappiness. Until today, he had avoided eating with his hands. So faced with the challenge now, he wasn't faring well. Regaining some of her composure, Mama replied, 'Your Highness is truly kind but Mr. Coquettish does most of the teaching. He is very patient.'

The Zamorin turned his attention to Mr. C. Looking at the cubes of potatoes that had been piled on the side of his leaf, the Zamorin said, 'You don't like potato, Mr. Coquettish?'

Mr. C shook his head vigorously, his cheeks retaining the deep red colour.

Carly was astounded by the *chamandi*s and stews. 'Your Eminence, for a Buddhist, vegetarian food is a compulsion?' she asked.

The Zamorin was a Hindu. Even I knew that.

He paused and looked at Mama, who had become quite pale, and remarked light heartedly, 'Hinduism confuses its own followers. It is an umbrella of many traditions. To some Europeans, Hindus are Buddhists.' He smiled.

I liked the Zamorin very much. There was something honest in his attentiveness to the guests, to Mama and how he answered Carly with no condescension. Observing our staff's easy manner with the Zamorin, how he twisted Sound's ear, how he embraced Narayanan Kutty and Krishnan Kutty, the way he blessed Damayanthi and placed a parcel in Chandran's mother's hands, it was clear he knew each of them well.

We returned together from the *Sadhya*. It was a convivial bunch that made its way through the streets. Sound sang a Malayalam boat song. Chandran walked barely inches behind me. Carly chattered about her plans to go to the royal kitchen the next day. Everyone was in high spirits and so was the militant monkey who seemed to follow behind. In his hands was the extra *laddoo* he had indulged in.

—⟫⟪⟨—

Just beyond the jackfruit orchard was a clump of trees. Tied around each trunk was a red thread. That was not the only thing that made them different from the other trees in the Tharavadu garden. Planted thousands of years ago, they were home to the monkeys. The single monkey who had flouted the 'one laddoos per head' rule sat on the ground. He dexterously removed one morsel after another and dropped them into a hole. Several hundred metres beneath that hole, in stony surroundings, were relics of his forefathers—the Monkey people.

—⟫⟪⟨—

Colin

I was born Danny MacFayden. My Catholic parents worked as tenant farmers on a small parcel of land in Cork. While the native Catholics were poor and miserable, the English Protestants occupied seats of power and privilege. Every day was a struggle for food. I fled from Ireland to England and reinvented myself. Colin Coquettish was born.

'You don't like potato, Mr. Coquettish?' the Zamorin had asked me at lunch.

I sensed an unspoken question. Or perhaps it was my paranoia. Potatoes were a painful reminder of what I had abandoned. No one in the *Tharavadu* knew I was Irish and I wanted to keep it that way. I took every effort to hide it. But had the Zamorin known? Did I let it slip in the conversation we had in his library. I replayed it numerous times.

I had walked into the Zamorin's library by accident. The door had been left ajar. Inside were rows upon rows of books.

'He hasn't read all the books here,' I said to myself.

'He has read it double times,' Sound chirped.

'Are you following me, Sound?'

'No.'

'No one can read all these books in a lifetime. And it is twice, not double times, Sound.'

'Mebbe he have twice lifetimes, Mr. Cockshit.'

'He has read it twice.' The Zamorin interrupted. He had just walked in and had obviously heard our argument. 'Some even more.'

Sound and I had struck a deal at the library. In return for refraining from murdering my surname, I would learn the names of the books that the Zamorin was going to tell me about that day. So I paid very close attention and concentrated every nerve on the mind-boggling names.

There were the Samhithas: the *Rig Vada*, *Sama Vada*, *Atharva Vada* and *Yajur Vada*. Then the Upanishads, which simplifed the Vedas and then the Upavadas that covered medicine or *Ayurvada*. Next was the *Gandharva Vada,* a study of music and dance, the *Dhanur Vada* on military science and the *Sthapatya Vada*, a study of architecture.

Sound had no mercy. He said I had reduced thousands of years of wisdom into street snacks. 'It is Veda, Mr. Cockshit,' he said. 'Not *vada!*'

The Zamorin had shown me his collection of palm leaf manuscripts. 'You may have heard of them,' he said. 'The *Mahabharata*, the *Ramayana* and the *Bhaagvadam Puraana*; our children have grown up with these stories.'

'Do you believe in blue-skinned princes and ten-headed men, your highness?' I asked.

'Our epics are like the deep ocean. They have something for everyone. A child is fascinated by colour and sees what is right on the surface. Some probe further to what lies within. Others go to the very bottom to find the soul and the reason it was written. To each their own.'

'What category do you fit into?'

'You could call me a bottom feeder.'

'He said bottom,' Sound laughed hysterically.

'They are very old,' I said, a pathetic attempt at an intelligent repartee and also to change the topic before Sound said something scandalous.

'Yes. I inherited them. They have been in the family for generations.'

'How many generations?' I asked.

The Zamorin didn't answer. He closed the doors of all the cupboards that had been opened. 'What do you like to read, Colin? You seem well read.'

I felt my chest swell with pride. 'I like poetry,' I said. 'Can you recite a few lines?' the Zamorin asked.

My mind was blank. Keats, Shelley and Wordsworth had deserted me. I looked at the Zamorin's face. He was in no hurry.

'Come, come. Come O love,

Quickly come to me, softly move,

Come to the door and away we'll flee

And safe forever may my darling be.'

The words had arrived on my tongue without warning. They escaped from a place I had locked up. A deep sadness coiled around me and tightened its grip. A fraudulent smile remained on my face while regret spread through my heart. The Zamorin was underwhelmed. He didn't say anything. He had been expecting Keats and I had given him the rough translation of a Gaelic song, Shule Aroon. It was my mother's favourite.

I was certain there was nothing in our conversation that had given my origin away. The Zamorin could not have known that the poem I had recited was a favourite among peasants in Cork. I convinced myself that there was only one rational explanation: A man who has to fake his identity has to contend with the persistent paranoia of being found out.

In my first week in Calicut, I had stayed with a lieutenant in his lavish twenty-five bedded bungalow and we had connected. Since then he had been away for almost a year but our friendship had rekindled recently over drinks at the Cosmopolitan Club.

The lieutenant was respectable and dignified. In his many years of travel with the British Empire, he had acquired an incurable affliction. It had incubated within while he travelled through Egypt, China, Hong Kong and Persia. But in the last year, the fever had taken hold of him.

The first symptom had been his hoarding of unreadable books, unintelligible parchments, withering scrolls, an army of broken statues, baffling reliefs and friezes and shards of pottery. The second more serious symptom, into which I had been conscripted, was the formation of the Chapter of the Asiatic Society in Calicut. It was a society that would devote itself to the study of Indian History by acquiring all manner of antiques. The original Asiatic Society had been founded by Mr. William Jones, in 1784 and attracted scholarly fellows. Membership to the lieutenant's society, on the other hand, was extended to peers, politicians, building and railway contractors, museum curators and businessmen. In short, it was a society that was amiable to my career plans.

The lieutenant had a steady supply of ancient artefacts that he exhibited during these meetings. I remembered the jewelled turban of a king that had been auctioned in one of those gatherings. The discovery of the vanquished king's blood stain on it had increased the bid. It was taken to England to sit in the morning room of a cotton merchant for six thousand pounds. There was conversation of how the price of a sacred crown of Shiva had remained unbeaten. It filled me with a surge of optimism and hope at my prospects. A percentage commission on each of these sales would make me a very rich man. I had found a perfect private venture but it needed to wait. There was the civil service post that I needed to achieve first.

I had put myself on a clock. The target I had set myself was a writer's job, which would lead nicely to a civil service posting. Writer jobs were on the path of extinction and there were only a few in the offering. I worked like a fiend, stretching myself between a teaching substitute at a missionary convent, doing odd jobs for writers in the administration office, running errands for the lieutenant and his contacts and earning my boarding and lodging at the *Tharavadu* by teaching in the evenings.

I drew inspiration from the railway service that started its life in 1825 in England. It was brought to a country that couldn't be more different—thirteen times its size and thirty times more dangerous, complicated further by the dense jungles, wild animals, venomous snakes and deadly climate. The officers of the Company, who pursued the railways in India, were gallant and ambitious. Motivated by these pioneers, I powered on too.

Some natives were so excited by the advent of the railways that they named their children after the trains—like Achyuthan Kabir Joseph, the first secularly-named native to pass the Indian Civil Service exam. He named his daughters Sahib, Sindh and Sultan after the three engines. There were those, like N Kutty, who bordered on obsessiveness with an unquenchable thirst for railway trivia. He waited for my updates on the railways like a parched dessert for rain.

'Sir, the Peninsular Railway is extending a line from Bombay to Kalyan? And then to Pune? How will it navigate the Bhor Ghat? It has an ascent of 1831 feet.'

Such was his insatiable thirst and enthusiasm that I found myself going out of my way to find details of the gauge, the length of the lines, the type of locomotives and where the next line was planned. He absorbed it all with great satisfaction.

But to most natives, the railway was akin to the arrival of the devil. The temples were doing brisk business with an increased offering to deities. Soothsayers and astrologers were consulted and all manner of charms and potions were administered.

A poem I had written made me very popular at the Club:

Here comes, Steam Loco, the Sly devil

Bringing Chaos, Disorder, Noise and Peril

'Can't you see you're Raavan,

A ten-headed demon.

To this land, you bring modernity?

Good heavens, what insanity!'

Let us stop it in its tracks

Before it does any more damage.

Filling People's heads with ideas of

refinement and good passage.

Such vile contamination

Is development and progress—

Order and organisation—that station in Hindoostan?

Surely, Sir, you can't be serious?

A single bud had emerged. It would bloom soon. Colin opened the cupboard door to let the light in. He did this religiously. Every time he did so, he held his breath, worried that his breathing would damage it. He was not a horticulturist but he could recognise the smell of the bloom anywhere. On the day of the Zamorin's lunch, he decided to break his vow. Now the potatoes were innocent. They were not to blame for the famine or what it did to his family and thousands of others in Ireland. They didn't need to carry his guilt. Nurturing this plant thousands of miles from its native place would be a penance for the regret he felt.

Sarah

'How did the man get injured, Papa?'

'Which man, Sarah?'

'The man who was saved by the monkey people.'

'Oh, the man in Shu's story? He was poisoned.'

'By whom?'

'It was a demon. It killed animals and plants. It poisoned the air they breathed and the water they drank. '

'I don't like demons. Papa, can you continue from where we left off?'

'The Seer didn't tell his people the whole truth.'

'What truth?'

'The truth about the vision he had.'

'So there wasn't going to be a cataclysm?'

'No, there would be devastation on a huge scale. But his vision had been confusing. A gold deer had spoken to him. Trees, animals and birds too. They asked for help.'

'The deer spoke?'

'Yes, but that wasn't the strangest part. The people of Meluhha would cause the destruction.'

'What?'

'The Seer couldn't understand it either. The people loved Meluhha. They were peaceful. There hadn't been a war in a thousand years. But his visions had always come true. That is why he had to go to the forest to understand it.'

'Papa, if he knew it was the Meluhhans who were going to cause it, could he have not stopped them?'

'He didn't.'

'Are you saying that he could have but he didn't?'

I had the strangest of dreams. In the beginning, it was mainly my father. Him telling me stories, him at the writing desk but in the last few days glimpses of a strange land made unannounced visits. Village life flourished on the banks of a river. It's people wore strange clothes. Men, women and even children led busy lives. They were engrossed in building and moving. There was an inexplicable sense of urgency and the pace of activity seemed almost frantic. The recurrent flashes of the same images puzzled me.

My husband too vexed me with every passing day. His absences grew. We didn't know who James went with or where he went on these extended tours. He never talked about his friends and colleagues except Peter. Peter Charleston was a captain stationed in the Madras Presidency. His trips to Calicut were rare but when he did arrive, he never failed to bring a box of *laddoos* for the staff.

James never spoke of his employer. The Zamorin didn't seem concerned about James' long absences either. Maybe he had a lot more to worry about than one errant employee. The Zamorin owned vast expanses of land that were distributed amongst tenant farmers. Per the Permanent Settlement act, the Zamorin had to pay the East India Company a fixed amount from the rent paid to him by his tenants. The *Karkidakam* had been particularly bad and the harvest had been very poor. I didn't agree with the Act and did not condone the Company's levy on the Zamorin and other landlords. But I kept my opinions to myself.

Carly, who had readily accepted the Zamorin's invitation, had spent a day in the palace kitchen. She had been amazed by the military scale in which food was prepared in the royal kitchen. She had seen many tenant farmers carrying small parcels of food for their families. She had learnt that the Zamorin had been providing them with lunch since the onset of the monsoons.

Carly had filled her book with recipes of condiments following her visit. She also showed me a deep vermillion flower that she had collected and pressed within its pages. She spoke of a group of sparsely dressed tribals that had arrived during her visit to the Palace kitchen. They had brought a large number of baskets containing berries and flowers. She was besotted by their deep vermillion colour and I didn't blame her. It was unlike any flower we had seen before.

A few days after the lunch, Sethuraman, the Zamorin's guard came home with a message requesting I meet him at the Thalli temple. It was a puzzling request but a voice in my head encouraged me to go. I took Charlotte along.

Sethuraman had been waiting for us at the entrance. There was no sign of the Zamorin. He gestured to a door at the side that led to the food hall. We followed him up a flight of stairs and were greeted by a putrid smell. The hall before us was covered with mattresses that were filled with rows upon rows of emaciated people.

Groups of young girls and women were crouched beside the starving figures, feeding many of those who had no energy to hold a plate. An old man collapsed on the floor near my foot. I had never seen suffering on this scale at such close quarters. I grabbed Charlotte by the hand and left the building as soon as I could.

For many days after that, I couldn't sleep. The images I had seen haunted me. In England, I had been shielded from the squalor in the workhouses. I had made no attempts to venture out and do anything about it. Aristocrats didn't want to believe that masses of urban dwellers were miserable. We did not want to accept that the less privileged had reason to rise and protest—a sentiment that had forced their peers on the other side of the English Channel to take the path of revolution.

I went to see the Zamorin several times after that but he was never available. I wanted to know why he had invited me to the temple. The classroom sessions at home had given me purpose but now I felt small and worthless. I learned of the vast indigo plantations, which had become a great source of misery here. Private contractors had transformed verdant landscapes of paddy to satiate the growing demand for indigo—a profitable cash crop that was exported to England. Cultivating the crop had deprived the farmers of food and in the monsoon months, the suffering had been exacerbated. The fertile soil had been robbed of its nutrients because of the aggressive crop, leaving acres of agricultural land barren.

Some months after that visit to the temple, a couple of British officers joined us for dinner. They seemed agitated. They told us that entire shipments of indigo had been rejected on reaching England. The indigo had produced a vermillion dye instead of the expected blue. That was only the beginning. Overnight it had become a national and international calamity. Newspapers in England called it the Vermillion Blight which had spelt disaster for the Indigo trade and the businesses that had sprung up on the back of it.

W e had been walking in the jackfruit orchard. Charlotte had seemed shut off ever since the temple visit. The experience had shaken me up so her reaction was to be expected. I knew something else was eating at her and sensed I would find out. Her voice choked and her eyes brimmed with tears. She said she had seen Chandran at the temple that day and that Aaji had explained to her that he and Chandran had been working at the temple for some years. They served the food, cleaned the halls and bathed the rows of peasants who sought shelter and treatment. Charlotte had felt left out. She wanted to help too. As a little girl, she was horrified at the prospect of getting her hands messy. Now, she was undaunted by the misery and wretchedness and wanted to help. She was growing up fast. My 'calamity Jane' had transformed into a determined and compassionate young woman.

We were interrupted by a sudden rustling sound. Sethuraman, Aaji, Sound, Radha and Chandran appeared from behind the trees. They were clutching a bag each and were dressed in black from top to bottom.

'Would you like to turn indigo into vermillion?' Aaji asked hesitantly. It hit me then: Vermillion, the flower that Carly had pressed inside her book and Vermillion blight that had turned indigo to bright pink. I took the black cloak that Aaji extended to me and wore it without hesitation. Charlotte followed suit, her face a vision.

A group of youth had joined us. Men and women I didn't recognise but assumed were tribals given their attire. Some of them even carried a quiver of arrows on their back. The contingent wove its way through the darkness, grateful for the light from the lanterns. We headed towards the fields. Out of Charlotte's earshot, Aaji told me that they had been going on these nightly missions for some months and that this was one of the last ones to be harvested. He said no more. I couldn't contain my excitement.

The moon had crept behind the clouds, cloaking a building in dark shadows. This was the indigo depot. High up in these warehouses were small slats, which allowed for ventilation. It explained the presence of the small boys in our group. Forming a human ladder, the boys scampered up to the top of the wall and removed the slats, creating a gap that measured half an arm's width.

Sliding through the gap like a contortionist a boy scaled the wall inside the depot and unbolted the door at the front. The guards were fast asleep and to ensure that they stayed that way, Sethuraman held a bottle of clear liquid under their noses. When I asked where they had got it from, Sethuraman smiled mysteriously and said, '*Chetan* made it' as if I knew who he was talking about. I didn't dwell on it. There was far too much going on.

The indigo plants were harvested and left to dry in the depots. Within the next two days, its dried leaves would be separated from the stems. After that, they would be powdered and mixed with other compounds to form the dye. The execution of the Vermillion plot depended on the window of time between the harvest and the separation of the dried leaves. At first, our group of night ramblers had seemed like a crowd. But considering the extent of work that lay before us, the resources seemed stretched. The cut stems had to first be divided and tied into bundles of similar thickness, which occupied the energies of a majority of the group. The rest were tasked with filling the assortment of pots, vessels and vats with water from the fresh stream that gurgled only a couple of yards from the depot.

Sethuraman produced another bottle that was much bigger this time. It had a vibrant wine-like liquid inside. He poured a proportional amount of the deep vermillion liquid into a vessel and mixed it with the water. The bundles were all immersed in the liquid, at which point, the tribals began a catchy and infectious song and everyone joined in. The full moon shone almost golden and the mixing of potions and singing made it all seem like we were a part of a pagan ritual. The bundles were then removed from the dunking liquid and the dye shaken off over gunny sacks. They were then untied and replaced in the heaps in which they were first found.

We returned at dawn, exhilarated by our part in this adventure. I slept soundly for an hour, waking only when I heard Girija making her way to the shrine of the Tharavadu deity, where she lit the lamp to start the day.

'She is beautiful!'

'She reminds me of the deer in Shu's story.'

'The one with the gold coat? The one who came to the Seer for help?'

'Yes'

At first, it appeared out of nowhere. Its colours were vivid, like it had stepped out of a painting. The colours were unlike anything Sarah had ever seen before on an animal.

Its coat had the decadence of silk and the textures of a richly embroidered tapestry. The lashes on her eyes were long and dense, giving her an allure of melancholy. Her eyes were molten honey. The speckles were defined with its concentric circles of bronze and gold. The first time she saw her, she had been sure she had imagined it. Deer didn't roam in the corridors of houses. Yet there she was, in the courtyard of their house, helping herself to water from the brass bucket.

Chandran

I felt the cold metal with my fingers. I tempted its sharp edge into my palm. The gold filigree on the ivory handle had been smoothened by a century of sweat, grime and the bloodied hands of valiant warriors. I was holding the Marakkar dagger. It was an award the Zamorin bestowed to the Marakkars in the 16th century for their exemplary courage in battle. That dagger had been presented to my *amma* on the day of the Onam lunch.

The day had begun with frustration. The sweet box had been hidden in the almarah. I had lifted the lining at the base of the box and looked at the message for the hundredth time that day, hoping for inspiration. The message had been etched in wax and revealed itself when I brushed it with some coloured water.

The much-awaited message from the Captain had been delivered. At least I knew now when the next consignment would arrive. Fortunately for me, the ship had been delayed and I had been given more time. On the other hand, I did not have a plan on how I was going to communicate this to my team without arousing suspicion. There had been no news of Chacko and I feared the worst.

I couldn't take any chances of meeting my team directly. Any face-to-face meetings would endanger the group. I had to think of a way of giving them the message without anyone suspecting it. How was I going to do this? I was desperate and took my frustration out on the almirah. I kicked it hard and the satchel that was precariously positioned on top tumbled down. That is how I had found the dagger.

A thousand thoughts crossed my mind. Had the presentation of the dagger confirmed my father's admission into the esteemed circle of warrior elites? My heart swelled with pride and my eyes stung with tears. But amongst these exhilarating thoughts was a distressing possibility. Could the presentation of the dagger have been a posthumous recognition of Abu's sacrifice?

Abu's absence had created a void in my life, one that I had grown accustomed to. The question of his whereabouts had perplexed me. But I grew to accept the mystery, secretly hoping that there was a chance he would appear again. The not knowing had been painful and I longed for answers. However, I didn't think that closure could hurt so much.

I realised why *Amma* had trembled the moment she was presented the satchel. But I had been ignorant that day. My head had been in the clouds. I had studied how Charlotte's eyes glistened with tears when she laughed, the number of attempts she had made to sit cross-legged and the number of awkward attempts she had made to get up after lunch. I noticed how she flexed her fingers, making gestures as she worked out an elegant way of eating with her hand. Her banana leaf, and the carnage around, showed evidence of her unsuccessful efforts. While she waited for everyone to leave the dining room, I waited to lend a hand. With Charlotte's soft, warm and chubby fingers in my palm, I saw *Amma* through the partially closed window. I saw her take the satchel from the Zamorin. I saw her stumble while Damayanthi held her. And all along, I was unaware that *Amma* and I were bereaved. After twelve years of not knowing where her husband was, my *amma* had received a dagger as compensation.

Amma had changed since the lunch. She became a shadow. She lost weight, her skin became dull and her eyes were sunken. She didn't sleep and didn't have an appetite. But she was filled with resoluteness and determination. *Amma* was like an eagle, gliding through the sky with quiet dignity. Her stretched out and unmoving wings showed nothing of the emotions that tugged at her spirit. But I knew how much she hurt inside.

Amma found solace in Kalaripayattu. Before dusk, she would open the doors of the Gurukul—a responsibility she had taken over after Madhavan Nair's death. Until the school found a replacement, *Amma* would be the chief instructor of the outlawed martial art.

Our vermillion excursion that night had gone according to plan. Kutty Ettan's plans rarely went awry. Every detail was meticulously thought out. However this mission had been different. There was no test run and it was executed over eight weeks following Onam. Things could have gone wrong. Charlotte could have been hurt. Part of me was happy that she knew which side we were on but part of me was afraid. Our Cause was a noble one. We were proud of the roles we played. But some of us had paid a huge price. I had lost my father and I couldn't think of losing her too.

'Ready for muwic (music) practice?' Aaji said chirpily as he entered the room. Aaji and I were to support the vocalist who was going to perform at the monthly Carnatic music sabha. I was roped into Carnatic music lessons when we first arrived at the *Maradu Tharavadu*. It was the *mridangam* that really captured my interest. Aaji played the *ghatam*.

This evening's concert would be well attended and members of my team would be there too. The artist, Subramaniam Pattabhiraman, was a devout follower of Shyama Shastri—one of a trinity of gurus who had transformed Carnatic music. It was a composition in the famous *Shankarabharanam Raaga* that Aaji and I had to practice.

We arrived late for rehearsal. Ordinarily, I would have been trying my best to impress the vocalist. But today, my mind was exhausted. The discovery of the dagger had made me numb. Not having a plan was eating at me. My group was expecting their instructions. Though I was well versed in the *Shankarabharanam Raaga*, today it was proving to be insurmountable. My percussion recital was unable to cope with Subramaniam's mellifluous *chittaswaram*. My fingers stumbled over the simple rhythm of the *Adi Thaalam*. My team would tease me no end if they heard me perform like this.

It was then that it struck me. My group would be at the concert. I knew how to get their attention. With some help from the vocalist, they would get their instructions. This evening's Sabha would be a test.

'I hope he didn't suffer.' Soujanya looked ahead, at the pilgrims in the temple. Her eyes returned to her best friend.

Damayanthi nodded.

'If you had been there, maybe you could have saved him.'

Damayanthi smiled. She didn't say anything. She just put her palm on Soujanya's hand.

'Chandran was six when he saw his Abu last.'

Damayanthi was now staring at the pilgrims. She stiffened.

'Damayanthi, your eyes are ablaze! Is that Captain Matheson? Oh no. Look at his face!'

-➤➤◄◄◄-

4

A Concert, a Cypher and a Tattoo

Calicut, India 1854–1855

Charlotte

'Come here Charlotte. Let me show you the Scind Dawk,' Papa said one morning. It was strange to see him at home. He waved a letter bearing a red wax seal on it. The seal had the letters 'SCIND DISTRICT DAWK' printed on the outer rim and the East India Company's merchant mark in the middle. His eyes twinkled with a fascination for the stamp. 'It's pristine. No postal cancellations.'

He looked at my face, which was a picture of unapologetic disinterest. Papa persisted unperturbed. 'Now, look at this one,' he said, holding out another letter with a similar red seal. 'Can you tell the difference, Charlotte? It is a used stamp. You can tell by the black cancellation marks. But if you look really carefully, you will find something else different about this stamp. Can you spot it?'

I hadn't noticed anything different. I hadn't even looked.

Now, looking at the two stamps, the only occupants of the capacious drawer in Papa's study table, I regretted not indulging him. Papa had left. I had sensed the tension between Papa and Mama ever since we landed in Calicut. At first, I wondered at Mama's transformation and the manner in which she immersed herself in the English lessons. But now it made sense. There was a void in her life and she had been trying to fill it.

Papa was gone. The shirts that hung in his armoire had been removed from their hangers. He had emptied all the drawers of his desk but he had left the letters with the two identical Scind Dawk stamps.

I picked up the letters with their red circular seals and looked at the Scind Dawks again, this time straining to see the difference he had spoken of. Against the rosewood patina of the desk, they looked the same. I held them against the sunlight and noticed faint lines or dashes just above the letters on one of the stamps. I wasn't sure if this was the difference Papa had wanted me to see. The writing in that letter was in a strange language, English alphabets but unrecognisable words. I wished Papa were here. I returned the stamps to the drawer with a heavy heart.

Ever since our adventure with the indigo harvest that night, my heart raced. I relished the thought of countless unsuspecting British officials turned out in their vermillion uniforms. The Blight had become an economic crisis. Entire shipments of indigo had to be destroyed in England. Shareholders of various trading firms that had sprung up overnight were up in arms. The East India Company was being blamed for sabotaging the indigo harvest of private merchants. Mama had explained how the indigo business had been a profitable venture. Landed gentry and wealthy businessmen had wanted a slice of the pie. They herded into Calicut and other major towns in South India, bidding for lucrative contracts handled by the East India Company. The blight had occurred specifically in regions where private businesses had acquired contracts. But tracts under the ownership of the East India Company had been relatively unaffected.

To them it had seemed like the East India Company was seeking to chase them off in an effort to monopolise the trade and they weren't happy. As a consequence, the Company had suspended its railway ventures as a precaution—they feared revenge from their rivals. Shipping was delayed as well. While chaos danced within the administration and their revenue was affected, we didn't feel joyous at the victory. The scenes I had witnessed at the temple were a reminder of the number of lives the greed for profits had devastated.

On the home front, Radha and I had become firm friends. We went on daring jasmine-plucking adventures (daring because it involved climbing a parapet wall, which was 12 feet tall, to reach the vines that grew on a wire mesh). Radha had lent me her skirt and blouse that day. Mama knew nothing of this and it stayed that way. We strung the jasmine together with *tulsi* leaves for the temple; we made an efficient rice pounding duo, taking turns at the stick and singing. I mimed the words of a Malayalam song while Radha sang wholeheartedly. She taught me to use the granite rolling stone to grind chutney. In the process, I got chilli in my eyes and was blinded for almost an entire day. Then Radha became my walking stick. She made me rest my hands on her shoulders and we walked in that way, one behind another like a single compartment train. And then there was Radha's allure on the elephants. Just by clicking her tongue, she could get an elephant to stand on two feet and by singing one line of a melody, the elephants at the sanctuary would lift their trunks in synchronisation. The elephant sanctuary was a banana plantation that the Zamorin owned and was where old elephants from the temple spent their retirement.

One evening, Radha suggested we attend the Carnatic music concert the Zamorin had organised at the Kamala Vilasam. When we got there, the Kamala Vilasam was heaving with an excited audience except for one group, who were definitely not there for the music. A large group of English officers and Indian sepoys had dispersed into the audience. Their presence seemed unnecessary but it had become a frequent occurrence. Gatherings were never complete without a police presence. They even arrived at weddings. On the stage Aaji and Chandran were seated on either side of the artist, trying to avoid the piercing stares of the gathering. They fiddled with their instruments, pretending to tune them. Chandran played the *mridangam*, a two-faced drum, while Aaji's instrument was a clay pot. Damayanthi sat behind the vocalist and plucked the strings of the *thambura*.

The concert began and after an hour of stifled yawns and the strain of keeping my eyes open, I decided that Carnatic music was not my cup of tea. I looked around in wonder at the awake and alert audience. Whoever had come up with the idea of an afternoon concert had not eaten Girija's lunch. I was relieved when the musicians finally took a break. The drone of the *thambura*, the clapping of the *ghatam* and the effort it had taken to keep my eyes open gave me a dull headache.

Radha was in an animated conversation with someone sitting behind us. 'The Ragam Dhanyasi is an unusual choice for the *kutcheri*,' the young man told her. My ears pricked. *Kutcheri*? That sounded like a dish Girija would serve for lunch.

'What is a kutcheri?' I asked Radha in a whisper.

'Kutcheri is a Carnatic music concert. This is a kutcheri.' She whispered to me.

89

Radha returned to her conversation with the young man. He was handsome. 'I am sure Aaji said that they were rehearsing the Shankarabharanam.'

'Dhanyaasi is a morning *raaga*, not the conventional choice for an afternoon concert.' The young man addressed this to me.

'Is it a mistake?' The prospect of a mistake had suddenly made this interesting.

'Not wrong, just unexpected. You can see the audience is not affected.' Radha replied.

'But if Chandran continues with the dismal way he is playing, the audience might start throwing their *slippers* at him.' It was the young man's turn. He looked genuinely perplexed.

'Why?' Now, I was very interested.

'For every musical phrase the singer presented, Chandran has replied with the same monotonous five syllables. What is he doing?' Radha exclaimed with her hand on her head. 'He is making no effort whatsoever! What has gotten into him?'

There was evidently more to Carnatic music than thigh clapping, clatter and drone. There was a science behind the numerous oscillations and patterns. The never-ending syllables were not just a boast of lung capacity but were of clever combinations performed extempore. Radha explained the components of the *Kriti* and I made a conscious attempt to recognise the combinations when the performance continued after the interval.

I found respect for the *neraval*, how a single line with three or four words could be sung in so many different ways, still staying within the boundaries stipulated by the *raaga* and the rhythm. Although the language of the composition was unknown to me, I could recognise the distinct variations of the same line, which had at first seemed like annoying repetitions.

The man Radha had been speaking to got up to leave. But the concert hadn't finished. I was surprised to see that he was Aaji's age, maybe even younger. Radha had told me that his name was Madhusudhan and that he, Chandran and Aaji had learnt music together. It has been more than a year since Radha had seen him. His family had moved to Thalassery.

'You are leaving so soon? Is it because of Chandran's dismal performance?' I asked him.

'It is indeed because of Chandran. He has instructed me' He chuckled. I had no idea what he was talking about.

Captain Matheson

'How many constables are stationed outside the gate?'

'Twelve, Captain.' The young constable directed his gaze at the commander's chin. There were no signs of follicles. His skin was grey and his eyes were greyer.

'Anything suspicious?'

'No sir.'

'Are you sure?' His eyes were unblinking. Was there even an eyelid? The constable wasn't sure.

'Yes, sir. The crowd has been divided into six zones, each manned by five constables. Some children didn't want to watch the concert so they are playing in the orchard.'

'Where is the Zamorin?'

'In the orchard with the children.'

'You said there was nothing suspicious to report.'

'Captain?'

'Take them to the station.'

'The children? Their parents will be looking for them.'

'That is a good idea. Take them into custody as well.'

Captain Matheson strode into the police station with a smile. He was looking forward to the Interrogations where his belt would do most of the questioning.

'Bring the children to me and leave the parents in lockup.' 'Captain, I am very sorry.'

'Speak up, constable. I cannot hear you.' 'There has been an incident.'

'What incident?'

'It happened soon after the concert. An elephant uprooted a tree and wreaked havoc near the Maidan. Decision was made to take an alternative route through the paddy fields and alongside the Banyan forest.'

'Are you saying that my orders were not followed?'

'The children have vanished, Captain. The parents too.' 'Where are the men who escorted the children and parents?'

'They are not to be seen, Captain. They disappeared with the children and parents.'

'Disappeared? You want me to believe that? What will you have me believe next?'

'I am sorry Captain. That is what the lady said.'

'What lady?'

'The mad lady, Captain. She lives in the forest.'

'She is mad and you believed her?'

'Tell me, constable. How old is your son? Old enough to run a house in the absence of his father?'

'Please, Captain. I am telling the truth. The lady is the only witness. We were separated from the rest of the convoy because of the elephant.'

'I want to speak to her.'

'Yes, Captain.'

'Bring her in.'

'What is your name? WHAT IS YOUR NAME?'

'I heard you the first time. It is a waste of time.'

'What is a waste of time?'

'How is my name relevant?'

'You speak English.'

She laughed. 'Look around you, Matheson. Every native here speaks at least two or more languages.'

'You will address me as Captain.'

'You are wasting your time.'

'I will have you skinned. Every dirty tooth in your dirty mouth will be plucked out. You will be hung upside down and your limbs pulled until you learn your place. And then everything will be relevant. '

'You want to know where the children and their parents are?'

'Yes.'

'I won't tell you that. But I will tell you where you can find the missing hawaldars. Are you interested?'

'Where are they?'

'Have you heard of the Banyan forest?'

'No.'

'You lie, Captain. Your constable told you about it.'

'How dare you?'

'Your constable told you that the route taken was through the paddy fields and the Banyan forest.'

'How do you know what he told me?'

'Again, you are wasting your time. Look in the Banyan forest. Hold on to your horse.'

'What do you mean by that? Is that a threat?'

'I shall leave now.'

'We shall see about that.'

He grabbed her arm. A searing heat travelled through his palms and he jerked back. He noticed the pattern on her skin for a fleeting moment. Her pupils shone black, blue and silver. He was momentarily blinded. When he opened his eyes, she was gone.

'Constable, gather the men. We leave for the Banyan forest.'

⸺➤➤◄◄⸺

It was dusk when the men slowly approached the thicket of trees. There was a gurgling in the distance. Birds sheltering on the branches above were unmoved by the arrival of the dozens of men who shouted for their missing colleagues. They were dwarfed by trunks as thick as churches. Their enormous roots were like the thousand pillars of the Mezquita.

A hawaldar astride a horse shouted, 'Stand back, Captain.' A shriek pierced through the still evening. The pillar-like trunks of the trees closed

95

in on the convoy. The wind picked up and leaves from the ground propelled upwards in a wave. Catapulted by the surging leaves, the Captain shot off his horse. The latter disappeared in a swoosh of whirling leaves, swirling branches and a great rustling of the wind. The horse had been swallowed into nothingness. Everything returned to its place and all was motionless. The birds remained settled. The three hawaldaars were still missing and now a horse was missing too.

--➤➤◄◄◄--

Colin

I had made the cut as assistant writer to the honourable East India Company. There was a probation period of six months after which I would be a bona fide employee of the greatest company on earth. I was popular at the Club too. I was the opening batsman for the team and was unanimously appointed mentor and guide to the new arrivals in Calicut. And to top it off, I was in the lieutenant's good graces. The get together at his home had left me brimming with optimism.

Gatherings at the lieutenant's house were convivial affairs. On this occasion, however, uneasiness lurked under the cordiality. The independent contractors, industrialists, engineers and other businessmen steered clear of the East India Company officials. The Vermillion Blight had polarised the two factions—the East India Company on the one side and the burgeoning group of independent contractors and merchants on the other. The charismatic lieutenant, however, proved irresistible to both groups. Aside from the frothing tension, there was no dearth in pomp and splendour. There was even ecclesiastical endorsement by virtue of the bishops and archdeacons that were present.

The gathering provided a glimpse of the state and the attendance of social events back in the imperial capital, London. The industrial revolution had created millionaires overnight. Merchants, railway and building contractors now rubbed shoulders with the landed gentry and aristocracy.

An archbishop and two archdeacons were a small representation of the large number of Methodists, the Baptists and Scottish Church missionaries that had forayed into various parts of India, bringing Christian wisdom to the heathen people of Calicut. It was a distinct reminder of a time in Ireland that I was well familiar with and was a memory I did not indulge.

The proceedings were opened by a small presentation on the work undertaken by Max Mueller. I wasn't familiar with his work but I knew that the man had divided opinions. Some in the Club called him an infidel while he was held in high esteem by the natives.

The session outlined the similarities between Sanskrit and the European languages that had inspired Max Mueller to arrive at the theory of the Aryans—travellers from West Asia, who he believed had invaded the subcontinent, bringing with them their horses, weaponry and language. No sooner had it finished, than there was a rush to the drinks cabinet. The Indo European language and its vagaries wasn't their idea of a merry evening and it wasn't mine either.

But the lieutenant refused to take the hint. He persisted with the now relatively smaller group and led them to the drawing room. Along the long wall of the room were a series of paintings that the lieutenant had arranged. He held up an oil canvas of a deer.

The subject wore a matt gold coat speckled with silver spots. Its eyes were big and beautiful. The many shades of green of the forest brought the gold out, making it shine in its emerald setting.

The seated judge had not been noticed until then. He had probably snuck into the room to escape the lecture on languages. He stepped up to the painting and kissed the deer on its mouth. Then he turned around and left the room, muttering the word 'Banoo'.

The lieutenant gestured to the servant to follow the judge. 'Poor Judge Jacob. He misses her.' He cordially explained that Banoo was the judge's Indian mistress and that she had died a week ago but how the deer in the painting reminded the judge of Banoo was a wonder.

There were two other paintings in this collection: A bow in a barren field and a congregation of people by a bonfire. They were random themes and I failed to see what the fuss was about. But I was no connoisseur of art. If the lieutenant had acquired them, then there was probably a good reason for it.

'The artist goes by EC. The attentive amongst you would have spotted a blue butterfly in each painting.' The lieutenant addressed his audience. They were in rapt attention.

A cotton merchant laughed loudly. 'Is the blue butterfly supposed to be a part of the signature?' He laughed again. 'A male artist batting for the opposite side perhaps?'

'Why? Couldn't it be a woman with the initials EC?' asked the lieutenant, interrupting the merchant's laughter.

To this, a few scoffed. 'A woman artist!'

The Lieutenant chuckled. 'The themes of the three paintings puzzle me. I have an instinct that they are connected but then again what could a deer have in common with a bow and a fire sacrifice?'

Only a few paid heed to the Lieutenant's words. The appeal of the imported Madeira proved impossible to resist.

As guests made a beeline to the drinks cabinets, the Lieutenant returned his precious paintings to his room. The intellectual part of the day's proceedings was well and truly concluded. Glasses clinked. Decanters were fast emptied. The servants couldn't keep up with the demand for alcohol. Platters of fried fish, tureens of soup and roasted cauliflower were ignored. Jugs of water could not be replenished quickly enough. The plentiful bottles of exclusive Spanish imported wine were soon emptied. Madeira started to make her intoxicating way around the room. She loosened the people's tongues and reduced their inhibitions. She was just getting started.

A drunken company official spilt a glass of red wine on the white suit of a distinguished industrialist. The suit turned a shocking red. 'I've just done a *Vermillion* on you!' His harmless attempt at a joke set off the spark. An altercation followed. Even the cassocks of the archbishops weren't spared. Goblets of wine were emptied over one another.

It was fortunate that N Kutty had told me about the large delivery of whisky made to the lieutenant's house just days earlier. (N Kutty always had useful snippets like this). Using more alcohol to dowse the alcohol-induced scuffle wasn't inspired thinking. But it was all I could come up with to defuse the tension.

I headed to the servants' quarters at the back of the property, hoping the package would be stored there. The servants' quarters had altered from the last time I had seen it. In a rush to break the scuffle inside, I hurried back with two heavy kegs of whisky. The warring factions were placated by the expensive and potent spirit. It knocked some into a deep stupor and others into incoherent harmless babble. Those who could walk were escorted into waiting carriages while others were accommodated in the colonel's mansion.

I returned to the building to replace the empty casks. When I had stayed with the lieutenant, the quarters had been utilised by the servants. The building had expanded both in height and width. But oddly enough, no windows had been added. So it was, in effect, a two-storey building with no windows beyond the ground level.

I heard a faint throbbing at the back and went to the jaws of the room to investigate. There were many crates stacked that were yet to be opened. I assumed it was more alcohol. I discovered a door camouflaged in the same colour as that of the wall. It had no obvious handle. I looked at it for a long time. I would have left it had I not heard a cough and a chorus of continuous scratching. I pushed the door and found myself in another room. The orange glow of multiple oil lamps and the musky smell of sweat flooded out.

A group of men were seated at desks; they looked up in surprise and returned to work swiftly after. The scratching I had heard was from the movement of their pens on the parchment draped on their desks. They were engrossed in making elaborate copies of brown scrolls that had been draped over several standing easels.

I was taken aback by the inhabitants of the room. Apart from the silent industrious men, there was a legion of artefacts in different stages of packing or unpacking: Friezes that stretched from the ceiling to the floor, oriental vases and rows of chiselled statues.

I heard a sound. It filled me with a strange fear. The lieutenant appeared with two men I had never seen before.

He looked at me, surprised at first. But soon, he smiled. I still had a cask in my hand. He understood immediately.

'Colin, the whisky worked. Splendid idea. How many drunks did you have to displace?' he asked. The fear dissipated. He wasn't angry that I had trespassed.

It had been an afternoon of exertion. I had helped two into the guest rooms upstairs. Half a dozen I had helped into carriages that I had organised. N Kutty had been at the tea stall not far from the lieutenant's house. With his help, carriages had been summoned expediently and the feuding tribe disbanded. For the second time that day, N Kutty had come to my rescue. Not that I needed rescuing but he had a habit of turning up when there was a need for reinforcements.

'Glad to be of service,' I answered, suddenly feeling flushed as a result of the pride I felt and the heavy lifting that had started to take a toll.

'Introduce us?' asked the other man who had been standing behind the lieutenant. He smiled yet it seemed like his mouth had been drawn and stuck on his face. His eyebrows were perfectly groomed, like the bushy tail of an English squirrel. His eyes were lifeless with their solid grey irises.

'Captain Matheson, this is Colin Coquettish, assistant writer and a dear loyal friend.'

'Solid English name. Pleasure.'

'Likewise,' I said, trying to assume an air of nonchalance. Inside, I felt my heart skipping like a child. *Dear loyal friend!*

'Residence?' Matheson asked.

'The Zamorin's property on SM Street,' the lieutenant answered for me.

'A grotesque street,' he said.

'The house is not intolerable,' I answered.

'You should be out of there soon,' Matheson said. Was that an order I wondered. I looked away quickly. He had caught me looking at his fingers. There were no wrinkles on his knuckles.

'I apologise. I do intend to organise my belongings at some point.' The lieutenant had seen me assess the room and its haphazard collection.

Belongings. All these were the lieutenant's belongings? How rich was this man? It was while staying at the lieutenant's that I had become historically enlightened.

He had a collection of catalogues of antiquities that had been neatly illustrated and labelled, with the prices underlined. Suddenly, my mind was inundated with the possibilities. Master Secretary to the lieutenant could be a lucrative career opportunity.

'Have you seen a beautiful woman with long hair and bronze skin? Do you know if she resides there? She couldn't have escaped your notice?' Matheson winked. I was unable to ignore the skin around his eyes.

'You mean Damayanthi? She dances beautifully.' I volunteered.

'Must be the one.' Matheson said as he considered the name. 'Damayanthi,' he said, looking at the lieutenant.

'Matheson, behave,' chided the lieutenant.

One of the natives looked up. Matheson went up to the man and appraised his work. He exchanged a word with his companion, who I hadn't paid attention to until then. He was a pot-bellied native with a bottle brush moustache, a compulsive *paan* chewer and it seemed he wore all the rings he possessed on his fingers. One by one, the other natives stood up and had their work inspected. The lieutenant stood by my side as Captain Matheson and his native assistant gathered the scrolls that had been filled with the intricate patterns.

'It was good to meet you, Colin,' Matheson said. 'Hope we meet again soon.'

The workers were led out through the door at the back.

Matheson and his assistant left too.

'Colin, you have been a big help. Thank you for sorting the mess earlier today.' the lieutenant said.

'What were the men copying? They looked like cuneiform.'

'Do you have those shipping logs for me?' the lieutenant asked. He hadn't heard my question.

'Yes, I have left them in your study.'

The lieutenant took out a wad of crisp £5 bills and put it in my hand. 'Sterling work, Colin.'

In the summer of sweltering heat, I felt the cool breeze of turning fortune.

The plant in his cupboard had shrivelled up. All the blooms had withered. Colin felt a foreboding in his being. He was puzzled. Life was good. He was successful. But inside he felt like he had made a big mistake.

Sarah

'Queer lot, these mixed bloods,' he remarked and burst into a menacing smile. The smoke and dim lighting of the Cosmopolitan Club added to the menace and made my heart burn. My eyes darted around, desperately looking for Narayanan Kutty. He had accompanied me to the Club but was nowhere to be seen.

'You didn't answer me Sarah.' I was stunned by his rudeness.

In the politest tone I could muster I replied, 'I am sorry.

Have we met?'

'I am Captain Matheson. I will call you Sarah.' he said, inching closer.

'Captain Matheson, I am sorry but I have to leave.'

'But you just got here. Why don't we sit and talk? Just you and me. Your husband seems occupied with some pretty business so I am certain he wouldn't mind.'

He was insistent and forceful and I found myself following him to a seating area at the far end of the room. I had no response to his comment on James. I was still reeling from it.

'Absinthe?'

'Over here, mixed blood!' he said to one of the men. He gestured to the steward to top up the solitary glass on the table.

The skin of the waiter was that of an Indian but his hair and his features were European. 'I don't mind sharing,' Captain Matheson said, taking a sip first and passing the drink to me. His smile was growing more sinister by the minute.

'Thank you,' I said, refusing the drink with a smile that I mustered from somewhere.

He leaned forward. 'I am interested in a woman,' he said. Sweat began to run down my back. 'Oh, don't worry, darling. She is not a patch on you.' His fingers rubbed against my gloves. 'She has a tattoo on her upper arm.'

He took my hand and traced the outline of a dagger on my palm. 'It's a dagger with a vine wrapped around it. Have you seen it?'

My mind raced. I had seen it. But all I could think of was how to get out of here. 'Yes, I have.'

He was delighted. He tapped my shoulder and my body shrank from his touch. He kissed my gloved hands. 'Thank you. Where can I find her?'

'At the house. Why her, if I may ask?' The words tumbled from my mouth.

'She has something we are interested in.' His tone was hushed. 'Shall I come by the house tomorrow?'

When I got home, I asked Damayanthi to leave the house at once. She didn't say a word but she hugged me before she left.

Captain Matheson arrived the next day just as he had promised. 'Where is she, my dear?' he asked.

Girija walked in at that moment. Her chubby arms bulged from her sleeves, revealing the artwork on her copper skin.

'It is not her!' he shouted and then immediately quietened upon seeing the expression on my face. 'Lady Sarah, I underestimated you,' he said and left immediately. From a distance, I could hear the doors of the gatehouse bang shut.

Girija returned, this time in her own blouse with its long sleeves. 'Shall I wash the design off, your Ladyship?' she asked.

'Yes,' I answered, thinking of my artwork with a sense of pride. I had seen it only once on Damayanthi's arm but remembered the flick of the dagger's handle, the precise number of leaves on the vine and then reproduced it on Girija's skin. I had got rid of the vile Captain but I knew that it wouldn't be the last time I'd see him. At least Damayanthi was safe. I had sent her away.

An unrecognisable being had taken over my faculties since that evening at the Club. I had shown strength I never thought I was capable of. I had heard that mental distress could alter a person drastically. I had seen James with another woman at the Club the previous day. Had the shock scarred me so much that it had transformed me into someone I barely recognised?

Once the thrill of my small achievement had worn off, the shock of the previous day's events sunk in rapidly.

James was supposed to be in Bangalore but instead, he had been at the Club with a woman. I wasn't supposed to be at the Club. I hated the Club. Going there had been N Kutty's idea.

The woman James had been with was beautiful. Dressed in the latest Victorian fashion, she carried herself with a regal air. James hadn't seen me. He was immersed in conversation with the top brass of the Company and various business tycoons. The woman had been by his side the entire time. I felt my mouth dry out and the ground beneath me cave.

It wasn't anger or betrayal that had surged through me then. It was the thought of how stupid I had been. I had believed that James' long absences had been work-related.

I longed to confide this horrible truth to someone. I wanted to pour out my sadness to Carly. I wanted to run back to England to my brother's protection and home. But I knew that though it might help me momentarily, I would never be able to control their emotions, pain and sadness. What was the point of inflicting sorrow on so many when I could lock it within and hope that it would pass? So I told no one and battled my demons on my own. Within, I clung to a hope that this could be salvaged.

I sought out stories of human tragedy because I wanted to have a good cry and indulge in an unguarded, unhindered surrender to grief. It was in the pursuit of human resilience that I stumbled upon the story of the Xing soldiers and inadvertently on further deceit.

Many years ago, when faced with imminent defeat at the hands of their enemy, Chinese soldiers and officials of the Xing dynasty refused to surrender. Instead, they had slit their own throats.

I had asked K Kutty if he knew the full story of the Chinese soldiers and he didn't disappoint. The British had developed a taste for Chinese silks and tea. Silver was the only payment the Chinese accepted. Silver, being non-renewable and with British bullion reserves fast depleting, the resourceful Company, with the help of native merchants, set in motion a new plan. The Company imported tea on credit, which was balanced by the export of Indian-grown opium. The smoking of opium reduced a vast majority of the Chinese population to desperation and incapability. The Chinese authorities made opium trade illegal. A year's supply of opium was dissolved in the sea by the Chinese officials, which led to the Opium Wars. When the British occupied Dinghai, not a single soldier surrendered. They committed suicide by slashing their throats.

Krishnan Kutty had rattled off the names of the private firms that engaged in the opium trade and the firms that had set up opium factories in Hong Kong. I recognised one of those names: Sir Joshua Burtenshaw, the owner of Burtenshaw & Co., was a family friend and grandpa's business partner. I had never shown any interest in our family's business affairs and my brother always said that I should not worry my head with matters of business. I knew our family had made its fortune through trade in the Far East. But a truth was beginning to emerge— one that my heart didn't want to accept—about my family and its connection to the opium trade. It made me feel sick.

I wasn't sure about anything anymore. It was as though my life had been an elaborate masquerade. The most important men in my life: my father, my brother and my husband, had suddenly become complete and utter strangers. I was consumed with guilt for the role my family had played and the havoc it had caused in China. My heart was broken because of my husband's deceit. I was clueless about how to make reparations and move ahead. I was disturbed and preoccupied; peace of mind had become a distant dream.

I found a partner in my grief in Soujanya, Chandran's mother. In those tired eyes, I saw an unmistakable emptiness.

I knew that within that resilient exterior was a spirit in turmoil. Ever since the Onam lunch, Soujanya had shown a more serious and quiet nature. But despite her inner battles she had stepped into the shoes of the principal at the Gurukul. I had dropped in one morning on my way to the Temple. I was mesmerised by her skill and grace. She made the martial art form look like a dance. Swiftly and gracefully she tackled four students in quick succession and flipped them so they landed flat on their backs. I felt overwhelmed with respect and admiration.

I had two paths before me: One was to wallow in guilt and heartbreak and let life pass me by; two, I could bury the hurt and move forward like Soujanya.

The lessons at the Tharavadu gave me purpose.

The fidgety and lively Tipu boys arrived in my classroom like an uplifting breeze. The Zamorin had requested that I teach them the basics of English and Mathematics. 'Their minds are sharp and their eyesight exceptional,' he had said.

I wondered about his unusual remark on their eyesight. But knowing the Zamorin, I was sure his words were not without significance, like his version of the Ramayana that he had shared with me. The Zamorin had not invited us for the traditional Onam feast that year. Instead, he had asked us to join the Ramayan recitation instead.

'It is a custom to recite it. Generally, just for the month of Karkidakam. In the Padmini Palace, we recite it on the day of Onam too.'

'I have heard it being recited at the Thali temple,' I said, much more vocal than I had been when I met the Zamorin first at the eventful Onam lunch.

'Yes, ours is slightly different.'

'Different? A different Ramayana?'

'Put simply, ours starts where everyone else's ends.'

'From the descent of Sita?'

'Yes, Saaru.'

'But that defeats the purpose doesn't it?' I asked.

Had the Zamorin called me Saaru?

'Why do you say that?' he asked kindly.

'If the intention is to instil strength and grace during the particularly harsh season of Karkidakam, shouldn't the more joyful parts of the Ramayana be recited?'

'You say grace and strength. What could convey grace and strength more than sacrifice for the greater good?'

'I don't understand.'

'What if I told you that Sita wasn't a queen but stood for the wealth and accomplishments of a nation. Rama was not the name of one man but the name of a loyal brotherhood.'

'What about the ten heads of Ravan?' I asked.

'Man's ten vices that take a glorious nation hostage.'

'And what is the sacrifice you speak of?'

'It is the price that was paid by mankind to release the motherland from the clutches of the ten-headed demon.'

'And the descent of Sita?'

'All that was sacred, precious, good and noble was worshipped as the Goddess. It was also buried within Her for protection.'

P apa had said that I was named after a great river—the river Saraswathy. To everyone else, I was Sarah. There were only two men who had ever called me Saaru. One was my brother and the other was the man who had rescued me from death when I was a young girl. And here after so many years, the Zamorin had called me that.

It was on the day of the recitation that I noticed the image carved on the Zamorin's coral ring. It was the outline of a dagger with leaves entwined around it. The same motif tattooed on Damayanthi's arm. I recognised it because of the stories I had been told. My papa had said that it was the insignia of the Guardians—noble men and women who had sworn an oath to protect an ancient treasure.

On the one hand, was deception—my grandfather and father's links to the opium business—and on the other hand, a motif from my father's stories. I believed in the truth of the stories, not because I knew for certain they were true. I believed it because I needed it to be true for me. My life depended on it.

When it felt like all was falling apart, it was what I clutched onto with fervent hope and willed, with all my being, to be true. And so the Guardians in my father's stories were not shadowy heroic figures. They acquired flesh and bone. It was the reason why when Matheson had asked me about the tattoo on Damayanthi's arm, I had taken a leap of faith and protected her in the only way I knew I could.

—➤➤◆◀◀—

'I know I can't stop you but take this with you.'

'An egg?'

'No ordinary egg.'

'Who does it belong to?'

'Only time will tell. I inherited it.'

'Is this a mascot?.'

'Something like that.'

'Of all our conversations, this is the most surreal.'

'Really? Not the story of Meluhhan flying machines?'

'You are right. The Vimana is hard to beat.'

They laughed. They had met as students in the cold, stone halls of Cambridge. Two decades had passed but it had not affected the vivacity of their camaraderie.

The Earl and his three ships headed out of the port of Calicut. Six months later, the ships docked at the Felixstowe harbour. To receive the ship at the port was an aunt and her two wards, a girl who wore metal callipers on her left leg and a her brother who was a few years older. They held each other's hands tightly. Behind them was a hearse drawn by four horses on a jet black polished carriage. They had come prepared.

A coffin was carried on the shoulders of four crew members, who made their way out of the ship.

Inlaid on its ebony cover was the shape of a dagger and climbing ivy.

Unknown to the humans on the port, from the deep waters of the Felixstowe port, a hatchling swum to the shore. It did not relish the salinity of the ocean. It preferred the tropical waters of the subcontinent where its forefathers had thrived thousands of years ago. It waited until the cover of darkness to lumber into the forest to grow and rest. It would remain in the forest until it was time for it to make its next big journey.

Chandran

I could see a group of kids running alongside the waves. Some dove straight in while others hung back, more cautious. The sea was in one of her happier moods, not very different from the last time we had been to the beach.

That day, only a few weeks ago, we had set a new precedent for wedding dressing in Calicut. The sand had clung to our legs, the salt plastered to our cheeks, our hair matted with sea water and clothes dripping wet. We had, in this fine condition, graced Juma Hall for Fathima's wedding.

Since Colin was away, it had been her Ladyship's idea that we all have picnic in the beach. We had conveniently forgotten about the wedding. It was only when we were wading in the water that Aaji came to inform us that we were wanted at the Juma Hall. Our arrival coincided with the arrival of the bride's party. Amongst the elegantly dressed aunts, uncles, cousins and friends, we looked like ruffians, all except for Charlotte and Radha.

The wedding had been beautiful. Fathima and her groom had known each other as children. They seemed genuinely happy and were oblivious to the stares of the guests, most of whom they didn't know. After the wedding, I carved Charlotte's name on the jackfruit tree in the orchard at the Maradu Tharavadu. I couldn't bring myself to write my name against hers. If there was the remotest chance we could be together, I didn't want this to jinx it.

'Decode *this*, Chandran.' Aaji interjected into my daydream.

I took the piece of paper from Aaji. It must have been one of the letters *Kallan* Tipu had decoded in Bombay. The boys were all called Tipu. Kallan Tipu was the naughty one and hence the prefix *Kallan*. A group of fifty soldiers had escaped Shrirangapatnam when it fell to the British. All boys born after were named Tipu as a mark of respect to their king. Besides the name, this particular group had one thing in common: brilliant eyesight—a skill crucial to their mission.

The boys were employed at the India Tiffin Rooms, just outside the East India Administration offices in Bombay. The Company offices in Bombay received large volumes of post, of which a large number were from the state of Sindh and bore the Scind Dawk Postmark.

These letters were temporarily stored in the mailroom before sorting and distribution. The sorting occurred in the afternoon, giving the boys a small window to perform their task. During their rounds serving tea in the morning, a handful would gain entry to the mail room and scan the mail for stamps with the engraved cypher. The coded message was embedded within the contents of the letter thus marked. Once the Tipu boys extracted the message, the letter was returned to the mail room.

Some months ago, Aaji and I had overheard a conversation at the Tharavadu. There was another person in the kitchen. But it was only Girija and Kutty Ettan's voices we could make out distinctly.

'He saw Damu at the temple. I think he recognised her.' Girija had said.

'She will be safe. I will manage this.' Kutty Ettan continued. 'Be strong. There is just one big task left. Then all our boys will be back. We will double up on the security here. For now, however, we stay alert...'

'The boys have been in Sindh for more than four years now,' Girija spoke softly.

'For this final job, they will be joined by others.' The three then left the kitchen. Girija had said four years. We had been engaged in receiving shipments at different beaches dotted along the Malabar Coast for four years. The weekly Carnatic music performance had become the means of communicating shipping schedules to my comrades. The *Taalam* gave them the time and the *Keerthanas* and *Kritis*' lyrics discretely altered to convey the location. Packages had been picked up from various beaches and hidden overnight in safe houses. That was our role in the operations. The next morning, the packages would disappear. It didn't need a genius to know that these tasks were linked and there was something much bigger afoot. Someone was conducting this symphony and held all the links that we couldn't see.

The Tipu boys left their translated messages with the proprietor of the India Tiffin Rooms but where the message went after that, no one knew. We got our orders from Kutty Ettan but we didn't know where he got his orders. The packages we hid in the safe houses were collected by someone. But we didn't know who. The chief composer and architect was obviously a person of immense intelligence and influence. I had a gut instinct that he was someone we knew very well.

From the conversation we had overheard between Girija, Kutty Ettan and the third person, Aaji and I had a strong hunch that all our work was related to the effort in Sindh. The Scind Dawk was the postage mainly used in this province and the coded messages were probably related to the progress of this undertaking.

Aaji and I were convinced that the shipments we received comprised of whatever the boys at Sindh were involved with—the conversation we overheard had alluded to that. We could only wonder about what it was. Aaji and I secretly hoped we would be worthy enough to join the group in Sindh.

Damu's involvement in all of this had caught us by surprise. But she was, on consideration, the perfect candidate. Her innocence, her quiet nature and her talents as a dancer had apparently been the perfect camouflage. But now it seemed that she was in danger.

I looked at Aaji. He seemed preoccupied. 'Do you think Colin works for them? The enemy?' asked Aaji, suddenly looking anxious.

'Why do you ask that?'

'He followed me. You know the day I didn't attend *Kalaripayattu*? I noticed him. So I decided to take him for a walk.' He smiled.

'A walk?' I laughed. But I was worried about Aaji.

'You know. I took him to the lighthouse, the *college* and borrowed the caretaker's clothes.'

Amidst the jokes, I knew Aaji had realised the seriousness of this development. Although he hadn't given away any of our secrets, it was apparent that Aaji was being watched. Kutty

Ettan had warned us that we couldn't trust anyone. There was every chance that Colin worked for the enemy though I didn't want to believe it.

I looked at Aaji's face. I saw disappointment. Aaji liked and respected Colin. We were interrupted by joyful shrieks from children playing in the water. Aaji and I looked around at our beach. To most, it was an ordinary beach. But 400 years ago, it had been the setting for a defining milestone in Calicut's history. Vasco Da Gama had landed here with his Portuguese contingent and discovered Kerala's treasures. Our Calicut had made its way onto western atlases. Our pepper, cloves and cardamom had become seasoned global travellers.

As the sun slowly stirred from the purple bed of the sea, we spotted the fishing boat on the horizon. Kutty Ettan had said it would take us to our destination. Our wish had come true. Aaji and I were going to Sindh.

5

Elephants and Birthday Coconuts

Calicut and Calcutta , India 1856–1857

Charlotte

Huge shadows played on a rocky surface under the Dutch factory. It was an unlikely place for a circus of men and animals to collaborate. No words were exchanged but a harmony of swishing trunks and human limbs worked at a pace like there was no tomorrow. Vats of tar were prepared and expediently layered on waiting surfaces. Tonnes of slabs were lifted and positioned dexterously by trunks. Several furlongs of frescoes unpacked and several furlongs more to go. They lined the corridors of the labyrinth underground.

The ritual started every day, exactly two hours after the evening prayers at the temple and culminated at dawn. A ferocious tiger's roar boomed from the forest to commence proceedings. It was brought about by a girl's single gesture. She would escape into the forest after her evening meal. During that meal, she cowered before her mother who extolled virtues of yam and carrot, the plumping effects of yoghurt and *pappadam*. But when she set foot in the forest, she transformed. The yam and the carrot plant bowed before her. The tiger acted on her instruction sounding the siren. Then the elephants arrived and the calves followed. A tinkle sounded the arrival of the newest recruit. The girl had helped him out of his enclosure and led him to the underground tunnels.

The entrance to the shrine heaved with devotees of different shapes and sizes. Little children threatened to climb the stairs that led to the deity's sacred chamber. Parents controlled their urge to spank them. Veteran devotees with ash smeared foreheads took up positions of importance in front of the shrine. They proudly exhibited sacred souvenirs from long pilgrimages on their necks and hands.

But the devotees and priests alike couldn't help turning around to admire the local celebrity. I was smitten too. Manikanthan had rocketed to fame because of his nightly escapades. The story went that one night the mahout had found Manikanthan's enclosure empty and had raced frantically around town, looking for him. Manikanthan returned the next morning, just in time for breakfast and oblivious to the panic. For a few nights after that, and in spite of Gopalan's (mahout) best efforts, Manikanthan managed to wander off. Ever since then, Thali temple had seen a surge in attendance.

It was Narayanan Kutty who had deposited me at the Thali temple. I hadn't minded the wait. My eyes followed the groups of frail people entering the complex where food was served to the poor peasants. The events of that day, when Mama and I had seen the scores of suffering, were still vividly etched in my memory. Mama had returned to the temple to become a volunteer ever since that day.

Narayanan Kutty finally emerged on the steps. He seemed displeased when he caught me staring at him.

Our manager was a strange man. Sometimes he would disappear for weeks. He would be flaunting a round potbelly one week and a few weeks later, he would be thin and sunburnt. It had been Girija who told us the story of Manikanthan. When I heard that Narayanan Kutty was going to the Thali temple, I had asked if I could tag along. Chandran and Aaji had abruptly vanished without a word, Radha had taken a vow to stay indoors and Mama had been very preoccupied. I wasn't left with many options and my own company was driving me mad.

As Narayanan Kutty and I left through the side gate of the temple, I looked back through the imposing gatehouse. Several devotees were looking back at the shrine to get one last glimpse of their deity; some genuflected at the steps of the gatehouse and others joined their hands in a closing prayer before they left. Some brought their problems and some brought gratitude. All of them carried a symbol of their devotion, either in the form of the ash or sandalwood smeared on their forehead, the flowers in their hair, the beaded chain or *rudraksh* they wore or even the *prasadam* that they had eaten. When seated in the outer hall, I had felt like I was intruding in their personal lives. But it had been a good way to spend a morning. When Narayanan Kutty mentioned an errand he would have to run a few months later at the Kadambuzha temple, I enthusiastically agreed to accompany him to Mallapuram.

M y birthday crept up on me. I woke up that day with a sinking feeling and not much to look forward to. Mama and I sat together in my bed. We both looked at the mural that occupied an entire wall of my room.

You could almost feel the movement of water in the lake. An exquisitely paneled corridor lay within the water. A blue butterfly was perched delicately on the top of the grey steps that edged the magical lake.

The face of a child leaned away from the step, peering into the water as if looking into the world within. The child may have been a girl or boy; it was hard to tell. But their dimples were discernible. Mama said her favourite part of the painting was the little child as it reminded her of me when I was young, with my dimples and my long dark eyes. At the bottom was the signature of the artist: EC.

Little did I know that I would cross paths with EC, that very day in fact.

An irritated and scruffy Narayanan Kutty turned up unexpectedly at our door later that morning. He announced the arrival of the cart for our trip to Kadambuzha temple. I wasn't prepared to spend my birthday on a bumpy trip to Mallapuram, which was half a day's drive away.

However, it didn't seem like a good idea to refuse Narayanan Kutty in his current temper, especially since I had, in a moment of madness, agreed to go with him a few months ago.

I stayed quiet during the ride there. It was the longest time I had ever remained quiet and my throat hurt. As we drew closer to our destination, I felt sick with disappointment. This was the worst birthday ever. Closeted in a coach with a stern companion wasn't my idea of fun. As though he were reading my mind, Narayanan Kutty began to provide a lecture on the architecture and symbolism of the Kerala temple in his bid to liven things up.

Narayanan Kutty likened the Kerala temple to the human body. The *gopuram* or the ornate entrance of the temple was the feet. The compound wall of the temple was the legs and the *naalambalam*, the complex surrounding the temple on four sides, the hands. The *pradikishina veethi*, or the path of circumambulation, was the stomach. The *Shri kovil*, or sanctum sanctorum, the head. And the deity that resided within, the human soul.

If he expected me to cheer up with that discourse, he was mistaken. My head began to ache. The one remotely interesting detail was how the Kadambuzha was different from other temples. There was no deity; the sanctum sanctorum contained a hole in the earth, which was supposed to have been created by the Goddess Kadambuzha.

A steep climb awaited us at the entrance of the temple. I looked around and evaluated my escape options. The coach had disappeared. Apart from the coconut vendor and the bullock carts, there was no escape.

I saw Narayanan Kutty return with a sack of coconuts. His ill temper had returned. A man followed him, looking equally sullen and carrying another jute sack of coconuts. 'It is all that idiot Chandran's fault,' Narayanan Kutty muttered under his breath. My ears cocked up in attention at Chandran's name.

'He pledges to break one hundred coconuts for the Goddess on this day and then promptly disappears.'

Following him as we mounted the steps, I took pleasure in Kutty's scowl and how his nostrils flared at short intervals.

Although I hadn't witnessed the rituals performed at Kadambuzha before, I had a basic understanding of the sequence of events. There would be the chanting of hymns by the priests, the swirling of illuminated oil lamps accompanied by the ringing of bells and the beating of drums. Today's ceremony was prolonged by the breaking of one hundred coconuts, thanks to Chandran.

When the ceremony was over, the priest handed me a tray of flowers, a parcel of sweet-smelling payasam and little packages containing sandalwood paste and ash. He blessed me by tapping my head gently with the sacred crown and wished me a happy birthday in English. I looked at the *munda* clad, semi-naked elderly priest, almost certain that I had imagined the words. But when he repeated the words and smiled, I was stunned. It was then that I found out.

Chandran's coconut offering had been made in my honour. It took a while to process this information. It wasn't every day that someone broke one hundred coconuts in my name. How had Chandran known my birthday? Why had he remembered my birthday? As I thought of the answers to the questions, I felt my heart race. My palms grew sweaty and my jaws tightened. I felt deliriously happy, beautiful and was overflowing with gratitude and love.

I bounced down the steps that only moments earlier had been the gateway to purgatory. The day seemed brighter and fresh, not stifling and torrid as it had moments ago. Even Narayanan Kutty seemed to smile momentarily. My being exuded affection for Chandran. I chuckled at his thoughtful gesture; its awkwardness and originality had bowled me over. A hundred coconuts! In the history of wooing and courtship, this was probably a first.

My head was in the clouds, dizzy in happiness. But not that dizzy to not notice the frantic activity taking place around a boarded up section of the temple. Narayanan Kutty had mentioned that a sinkhole had emerged in the old sanctum.

It had threatened to swallow the structure surrounding it. The inhabitants of the old sanctum were being carried away.

It was then I noticed a labourer hoisting a large painting on his back and making his way down the stairs. As the labourer waited for the bullock cart to approach, I stared at the unmistakable blue shape on the edge. It was a replica of the butterfly in the mural in my room. At the bottom of the painting were the initials of the artist: EC.

'You should rest.'

'I want to finish this painting. Butterfly, he calls me. Because my mind flits, you see. Always from one thing to another.'

'He says you are his spirited flower—fragile but determined, colourful but dignified.'

'The king can be poetic.' She breathed with difficulty.

'He is on his way. Do you want to hold on until he comes?'

'I have left him plenty to remember me by.'

'You drew them in your paintings?'

'Yes, in each one.'

'The blue butterfly is your favourite?'

'No, it is his favourite.'

'You didn't answer. Do you want to wait until he returns?'

'No, I couldn't bear to see him sad. Damu, you can take me away now.'

Colin

It was at a meeting at the lieutenant's house that Captain Matheson mentioned the arrival of the three East India Company directors.

'Why, Colin! You must go to Calcutta and meet the directors in person. I will write you a letter of recommendation.'

I barely slept that night. My mind buzzed with excitement. It was God sent. There was a civil service job that had just been advertised. I was not eligible to apply but the lieutenant had said that influence often worked. And when it was a director's recommendation, no one could refuse. I made several versions of my biodata that night, unable to sleep. Matheson had asked me to pick up the reference letter from him the next day.

'I have not forgotten your letter. But there is this bothersome piece of work that has landed on my desk. Frankly, there are much better things to do with one's time.' he said, looking preoccupied.

'Anything I can help with, Captain?' I asked.

'If you could it would be of great help. It is surveillance of a boy you know well. Just a few hours work and we should be able to clear this misunderstanding pretty quickly.'

The Captain looked at me and attempted a smile. It was still difficult to look into those eyes, those pupils fixed and unnerving. Matheson continued. 'I know you will treat this with the utmost discretion. Report back to me tomorrow. I will have a letter of reference ready for you by then.'

A nd so I found myself, tired and sleep deprived, hiding behind the tea shack just outside the Tharavadu gatehouse, waiting for him to appear. Aaji's day started a few hours after midnight. He walked down the beach road, which, even at this time of day, showed traces of activity. Aaji had first walked to the north of the beach to the French Loge, an area so named because it had once been leased to the French.

The factory had been abandoned and the neighbouring slums housed opium dealers and criminals. I was glad when Aaji quickly made his way out of there. He then headed south. The lighthouse had been a recent addition to Calicut. Aaji let himself through the front door and disappeared for almost an hour.

While I waited behind some rocks, I watched the ships prepare for a frantic morning. When he crept out of the lighthouse, Aaji had a bundle in his hand He sat on the beach for a while and greeted a group of fisherman who were preparing for their morning catch.

On the main beach road, past the Club, the *Pandikasalas* had opened for business. This stretch belonged to Mopilla merchants. Their *Pandikasalas* were multifunctional entities that served as a warehouse, residence and office. Horse carts and bullock carts jostled against one another while natives busied themselves, emptying sacks of grain and bundles of cloth. Horses that had just arrived from Arabia and Gujarat were herded together while horse traders carried out animated conversations with their customers.

Aaji wove his way sometimes stopping to pet the horses, sometimes peering at the crabs as they clicked against one another in their crates. Then he picked up a more determined pace and walked towards the St. Joseph's Church and vanished into its grounds. He reappeared with a guava in his hand and a few tucked into his pyjamas. Then he turned into St. Joseph's School.

It would be only a matter of hours before I would have to walk through those gates for my weekly class on Mathematics (I was substituting for a teacher who had been taken ill). After an hour, he emerged. The jaunt continued towards Kuttuchira Road which led to the busy Velliyangadi, the grand bazaar of Calicut and its nerve centre. Its main street was lined with shops selling everything from sweets, dates, bronze vessels and textiles to footwear. It may have been only six in the morning but I was ready for bed. Thankfully, Aaji seemed to have completed his tour for the day and headed back to the Tharavadu.

I had been meticulous in my report. Both Chanakyan and Matheson had remained expressionless. Their only remark was that my observations had confirmed what they had known all along. I was glad. I liked Aaji and felt satisfied that I had cleared his name. Matheson prepared the reference letter as he had promised. My heart thumped in anticipation. I was going to Calcutta.

'Nothing will impress the directors more than a first-hand observation on the state of education in Calcutta and recommendations for improvement,' he said. 'The directors want to see drive and focus. If I were you, I would focus my study on Black Town.' he said as he attempted a wink. The eyelid on his right eye collapsed and a stream of pale yellow fluid escaped through the corner. He removed a folded kerchief from his pocket and dabbed it; his eye didn't waver once through this ordeal.

I arrived in Calcutta, cock a hoop. Calcutta was Britain's imperial capital in India. The residence of the Governor General stood magnificent, bathed in the glory and power of the British Empire. Its honey coloured dome, marble hall and pillared ballroom dazzled all visitors. The vista of palaces on Chowringhee Street were each more exquisite than the last each built in the Palladian style, with pillars, opulent verandas and tiled corridors. I had admired the stupendous Fort William, which took pride of place in White Town. Built on the banks of the Hooghly River, it was a star-shaped fort.. Opposite it was the sprawling Maidan with its landscaped gardens.

But nothing could have prepared me for what Black Town had to offer. It was a maze of dark and smelly streets lined with godowns, ramshackle houses, dingy tenements and crowded slums. Disease was rampant due to stagnant tanks, open sewers and slaughterhouses that shared space with the settlements. No sane white man would be seen in these parts and yet here I was, determined to complete my task though my better judgement warned me of the perils.

In an hour, I was lost in a network of filthy lanes, each bordered by human excrement and abhorrent remnants of human cadavers. From a distance, I could see the smoke rising from the skyline of White Town. One of its Palladian palaces was being readied for an evening of drunken merry-making while I sunk deeper and deeper into this labyrinth of squalor.

Black Town reminded me of my homeland. Our land had been subdivided and poor tenant farmers slaved on their little parcels of land for their sustenance and livelihood. Potato was the chief crop; however, when the potato blight struck the country, we were propelled into a whirlpool of endless misery and desperation. The potato blight ruined the potato crops. A population that was already starving was plunged deeper into suffering and disease yet ships laden with Irish Corn were exported from our country.

With the failure of crops, my father and my older brothers had found employment with public works. However, as they were no longer funded by the government, there was no money earned. Food prices soared. Soup kitchens closed. Typhoid and cholera swept through the nation. Tenant farmers who couldn't pay rent because of the failure of the potato crops were evicted, making millions homeless and destitute.

My father succumbed to his injuries after a mugging incident and my older brothers boarded a ship that was sailing to America. My mother took my brother and me to several workhouses, which were besieged, and we finally found shelter in one. My younger brother didn't last long. He died of cholera. It was my mother who asked me to escape and take the next ship out of Ireland.

For years, I had felt guilty for abandoning my mother. I could have brought her along. Or I should have stayed. Perhaps I could have contributed to the Nationalist Movement if I had survived cholera, typhoid, the prolonged periods of starvation and the filth and squalor of the workhouses. As I walked through Calcutta's Black Town, I saw my mother's helpless face in each Indian woman and my little brother's pale face in every child.

When darkness fell, fear and dread gripped me. I collapsed like the pile of rubble around me, the odours of death and disease and the howl of wolves in the distance prepared me for my fate. If it weren't the wolves, it would be the natives who got me. I had escaped certain death in Ireland only to invite it in Calcutta.

An angel called Somesh found me. If it weren't for him, I wouldn't have made it through the night. Somesh had taken me to his home, an imposing building, which housed many generations of Chatterjees and functioned as a school during the day. Vidya Mandir had been set up to educate children from the nearby slums. Somesh led a team of five teachers, who had dedicated themselves to bringing education to the backward classes. A lively group of little girls followed the graceful Odissi steps of their dance teacher while another group studied Bengali poetry and literature. In the midst of the dark squalor of Black Town, Vidya Mandir was an oasis of culture, learning and preserving traditions that had been passed down for several generations.

The next morning, after a fitful night, I made preparations to leave the Vidya Mandir. Somesh took my hand and said, 'I was instructed to come and look for you in Black Town. You are alive because of this man.' I turned around to see Dr. James at the door.

Sarah

'So Shu **wrote** about the Meluhhans?'

'I've only told you that every night for the last year, my dear one.'

'Papa, you exaggerate so much. How did he write? Did they have books in those days?'

'Not books. But they used large leaves and stone tablets.'

'Stones?'

'Writing on stones meant they lasted so people like us could find it. But that wasn't the only clever thing. He commissioned a translation table, a steele..'

'How is that clever?'

'Many of the Mesopotamians didn't know the language of the visitors from the fascinating land. So Shu put together a table with Mesopotamian in one column and Meluhhan on the other so they could work it out.'

'Where is Shu's 'Steele'?'

'It was built, then dismantled, then taken on a long trip and then buried across the plains of Meluhha.'

'But what use is that Papa? The Stele would never be found!'

'There was a map Sarah.'

The mood in the Tharavadu was one of jubilation. It was as though the *Kutumbam* were celebrating a festival. Six months had felt like a year and now Chandran and Aaji had returned from their expedition to a jubilant reception. Charlotte was trying hard to contain her excitement. It was, however, the introduction of the tall, handsome stranger that evening that had largely been the reason for the gaiety.

'Your Ladyship, this is my father, Syed,' Chandran said, gesturing to the man who had his arm around Chandran's shoulders.

I looked at the father and son standing in front of me. Syed was a handsome man. Chandran had his height and his looks.

'You knew him as Madhavan Nair.'

Madhavan Nair was dead. What did Madhavan Nair have to do with any of this?

Chandran repeated the words slowly and deliberately. He scrutinised my face for a reaction.

There was a peal of laughter from the gathering. I closed my eyes and pictured Madhavan Nair. When I opened my eyes, Soujanya stood in front of me. Her face illuminated and she took my hands in hers. It began to make sense. I looked at Soujanya's face. The darkness had lifted and she looked years younger. Her beautiful eyes and sharp nose were accentuated by skin that had regained its shine. Her husband had returned. Even Chandran seemed more his age—more light-hearted, bursting into laughter and was all smiles at the drop of a hat.

Krishnan Kutty drew me aside and explained how Chandran's father had been forced to disappear fifteen years ago because of his involvement in an incident. It had been under Captain Matheson's watch. Matheson had sworn revenge. As a precaution, Syed had disguised himself as Madhavan Nair on his return to Calicut. His prowess in *Kalaripayattu* garnered him the principalship of the martial art school.

'What was this incident, Krishnan Kutty?'

'A robbery.'

'And Madhavan's 'death'?'

'That was because of the Thompsons.'

Krishnan Kutty went on to explain that Mr. Thompson—the previous resident of the Tharavadu—had misbehaved with Damayanthi due to which Madhavan had intervened. Although his intervention had the desired effect and the Thompsons had left the country, they could not forget the humiliation. In a recent reunion, Mr. Thompson had shared his experience with his old colleague, Captain Matheson. In doing so, he brought Madhavan Nair to his attention. Madhavan was a man of unusual height and physique. It was only a matter of time before Matheson would discover that Madhavan and Syed were one and the same. It was to throw Matheson off the scent that Madhavan Nair faked his own death.

'What did Syed steal?'

'A map.'

'Was it worth it?

'Yes. Syed would do it again if he had to.'

'Where has Syed been all this time?'

'He has been in Sindh with our boys.'

'But why has Syed come here now? Captain Matheson is here. He will find Syed.' I exclaimed heatedly. Seeing the happiness on Soujanya and Chandran's faces, I was fearful that this happy reunion was going to be short-lived.

'He wanted to meet you.' I was touched but couldn't understand why Syed needed to risk his life to meet me. I looked around at the gathering. Soujanya smiled back at me but I recognised the hesitation in her laughter. She was afraid of losing her husband. I knew that feeling. Captain Matheson filled me with dread too. He was a poisonous snake and I did not doubt that he had spies everywhere. There was another person I didn't trust in the Tharavadu but he wasn't a part of this convivial group.

It had been Narayanan Kutty who had forced my presence at the Club that fateful evening. I had seen him speaking to Captain Matheson later that day. Narayanan Kutty's long absences, his cloying familiarity with Company officers and his stern interactions with the staff had always made me uncomfortable. I didn't trust him. Getting straight answers from Narayanan Kutty was difficult. He had skirted around my questions like an eel when I asked him about the woman who had been with James and had dismissed any recollection of her.

That evening, we had an unexpected visitor. In James' absence, Peter's visit was alarming and I suspected the worst. It was strange that after all I had been through, I was still concerned and worried about my husband's welfare. Charlotte greeted Peter cheerfully and had been showing him the sketches in her scrapbook when I walked into the room.

'Hello, Sarah. You look well.' Peter was his affable self. The anxiety I had felt melted away. So nothing had befallen James. My heart calmed down but my fear turned into anger.

'Do I look well, Peter?' Charlotte left the room in a hurry, leaving her scrapbook behind. Peter stared at the book, unable to look me in the face. From his countenance, I was certain he had known of James' relationship with the woman. Although I felt guilty for taking my temper out on him, I couldn't make the effort to be amicable.

'Sarah, I know it hasn't been easy.'

'I feel like a fool.'

'Sarah, James loves you.'

'Where is James, Peter?'

'Sarah, it is not for me to tell.'

'I know about the other woman.'

'It is not what you think. Let me try and explain.' Peter paused and began pacing the room. 'Have you noticed Soundarajan's eyes?' he blurted.

'What do Soundarajan's eyes have to do with anything Peter?'

'His eyes are blue and his hair is brown with gold streaks.

He is mixed blood.'

'Why this sudden interest in mixed bloods? First, it was the despicable Captain Matheson and now you?'

'You met Matheson?'

'Yes, I did. The same day I saw James with her at the Club.'

Peter was seated now. His eyes looked desperate. 'I am trying to explain it to you, Sarah. Did you notice anything about the woman with James?'

'What are you saying?'

'James has a family here, Sarah. He–'

I had heard enough. I stood up and left the room in tears. James had a family? I couldn't bear it. The pain in my chest grew and I felt myself crumple into my bed. My cheeks were drenched with tears and my eyes shrank deeper into their recesses. I felt guilty. I always felt guilty after an altercation, even if it wasn't my fault. I wanted to erase Peter's last sentence from my mind. I felt sorry for the way I had behaved. My stomach clenched with nervousness and anxiety but Peter's revelation had been another devastating blow.

I may have fallen asleep for a few hours but I woke up with a start. Darkness had descended. I was exhausted but completely alert. I retreated to the armchair that James used and gazed at the pillared corridor before me. This was where James would sit for hours when he returned from work. Tears streamed down my face. Why had he done this to me and why did I feel so helpless? I stared at the door as though hoping for an answer. A fleeting glimmer caught my attention. It came through the slats on the doors that led to the *Kulam*. I looked at the doors. The bronze studs gleamed from the light of the moon and for a few moments, I believed they had been the source of the twinkling I had seen.

This time, it was clearer. A flickering of tiny wings was just about visible through the vent at the top of the door. I stood up and found my sight hindered by the roof. Returning to my chair, I waited, focusing on the spot. This time, her shape was clear. Her wings were an iridescent blue. She was slender and magnificent and the moonbeams shone through her tiny body. It may have been mere seconds but the experience had been uplifting. The heaviness in my head had cleared and I was filled with hope. It was just a butterfly but there was something magical about its appearance.

I stared at the doors that led to the *Kulam*, hoping for another sighting. It was then that I noticed the odd arrangement of the studs on the door. It didn't follow a pattern or symmetry. Squinting, I realised the studs were arranged to form the letters E and C. Could this be the same EC—the artist of the mural in Charlotte's room?

I remembered the blue butterfly in the painting and the image of the little boy with his olive skin and dark brown hair. The boy had reminded me of Charlotte when she was little. This house was revealing details I hadn't noticed before. Wasn't it Krishnan Kutty who had said that the house reveals what it wants you to see?

Krishnan Kutty's appearance at the door startled me. He was travelling with the Zamorin to Mallapuram because of a feud that had escalated between the Mopillas and the Namboothiris. I would ask him about EC on another occasion. He promised he would be back for the temple *Ulsavam*, which was only a fortnight away. I had been so preoccupied with recent events that I had completely forgotten about the great temple event that the whole town had been gearing up for.

'You saw her again didn't you?'

'I don't know.'

'She followed you. When you were at the indigo depot, you glimpsed her behind the trees and then she followed you home. She was there at the Club too, that day when you saw James and the other woman.'

'I am not sure what I saw.'

'Your dad told you about the gold speckled deer in the Seer's vision.'

'You think it's the deer from Shu's Tales?'

'The deer was the first animal that came in his vision. It pleaded. Other animals and plants and trees followed but it was the gold deer first.'

'But that is just a story. My deer has nothing to do with it.'

'It is more than a story, you know that. The deer is here for you.'

'What are you trying to say?'

'In the Ramayan, it was a gold deer that started the trouble. It was what led to Sita's kidnap.'

'But what does the Ramayan have to do with the Seer's vision?'

'Don't you see the parallels between Shu's tales and the Ramayan? The pivotal gold deer in both stories, the monkey people in Shu's tales and the Vaanaras in the Ramayan?

'You should go. You are stepping into my dad's stories. You are twisting them. There is no link between them.'

'There is and you know it.'

'Leave me alone.'

'I can't, Sarah. I am your thoughts.'

Chandran

'And this is a *pagadi*!' Aaji announced with a flourish. He strode along the length of the room, flaunting the turban and demonstrating how it had been a part of our uniform during our excursion.

We had gathered in one of the bigger rooms of the *Maradu* house, sharing stories of our adventures with Radha, Charlotte and Sound. After days of being jostled to the whims of the Arabian Sea and the Sindhu, our knees buckled, unaccustomed to the terra firma of the Sindh plains. Although Aaji and I had travelled, we had never ventured so far from home. We were experiencing, first-hand, the humbling vastness and incredible diversity of our land. It was my father who met us at the busy fishing village, some distance from the marshes of Kutch. But of course, I hadn't known it at the time. He had introduced himself as Mahendra Singh and spoke to us in Sindhi. His skin was pockmarked, his beard grey and he wore a large turban that was distracting.

'When did you discover he was your father?' Charlotte asked eagerly.

'Not until the very end,' I said. 'We were actually quite frightened of him and tried to keep our distance.' I looked at Aaji and he nodded vigorously.

It hadn't just been Aaji and me who made the journey from the far end of the peninsula. A dozen others had joined us from Madras and Mysore. Moreover, Aaji and I had been too busy absorbing our foreign surroundings to scrutinise our leader's features. Everything about this new land was so different from what we had been accustomed to. The turban was just one of the new things we had to learn. Another was mastering the language, Sindhi.

We lived like nomads, changing camp from time to time and seemed to choose the most uninhabitable locations for our base. We went about our tasks with military precision. Mahendra Singh wouldn't have it any other way. The first couple of days were arduous. In retrospect, it was training for the days ahead. We spent fifteen hours, rigorously brushing and scraping. It was unrewarding. During the practice rounds, a thousand granite stones had passed our hands.

Every pair of hands had to follow a meticulous procedure. The point of it was lost on us and the granite. Whoever brushed, then scraped, filed and patted a granite stone would know that it was as pointless as trying to get water out of stone. But when day three arrived and the first excavated object fell into our hand, the regimen and its purpose kicked in.

The object was a constituent of something large and monumental—that was what we had been told—but of what, we didn't know. The specimen was organic. Its surface was layered and its appendages were many and confounding.

No two were the same. The appendages interlocked. Some had cogs, grooves and sockets while others had wheels and ratchets. Its pattern intensified with ever rub.

Some had honeycomb hexagons and others had spirals and hypnotising patterns of butterfly wings. Some were covered with metallic feathers. It was like mother nature had imprinted herself on every one of them. No implements or cloth were used. That was the strict order. The sweat and oil from our fingers produced the polish and the lubricant.

Our fingers separated the appendages that had been glued together with the dirt. The specimens responded and forgave the clumsiness of our movements. The golden ratio of mother nature appeared without fail on the pattern on every piece. It was as though she had produced each one of them. Aaji recognised the mathematics in it. He never tired of marvelling at each piece.

We maintained an inventory of tools and equipment, every detail before and after our dig was noted. The dig itself had to be meticulous. Every tile, bone, seal and fragment was returned to its place in the earth; it was the peculiar specimens that we were after. After the meticulous cleaning they were transferred to bullock skin bags that were lined with hay and straw.

Some of our group were tasked with the transport of the bags to waiting barges on which they made their journey down the tributaries of the Indus. They were then met by larger ships at Karachi.

It was a few days after our arrival at a region with numerous mounds—we noticed an urgency in Mahendra Singh's manner. Our shifts doubled in duration. Hectares of land had to be excavated and objects retrieved. Aaji had lost his precious pocket tool during one of the digs but fortunately, it wasn't noticed because of the frantic activity. It was our leader's role to mark the site and prepare the site boundaries.

'But why the sudden urgency? Were you all in danger?' Charlotte asked.

'I think the letter informed him of an imminent threat,' I replied.

'These letters used the new four *anna* stamp which he received from Calcutta. The cypher was embedded in these new stamps just like the way they were in the Scind Dawks.'

' Scind Dawk?' Charlotte asked. Her face darkened as though the question had a much deeper significance.

'Scind Dawk is a postage stamp,' I answered. During our excursion Mahendra Singh would make a trip once a week to the administration office in Sindh, where he would steal a couple of letters designated for Bombay. He would pry the Scind seal open and slip a coded message within the letter, after which he would apply the indents of the cypher to the seal. The letters would reach the administration office in Bombay, where the Tipu boys would intercept them.

I noticed a pained expression on Charlotte's face. I wondered if it had to do with her father. There had been no news of Dr. James' whereabouts for months. I felt guilty and ashamed that I had forgotten her pain and anguish in the midst of my happiness.

The letters from Calcutta had been frequent and influenced our operation in Sindh. The most efficient way of completing our mission would have been to tackle geographically proximate locations consecutively. But there had been nothing logical about our approach. Looking back, the intensive reconnaissance and the arrival of the letter before our departure for the next destination started to make sense. Prior to commencing work at a new site, Singh conducted a surveillance of the area for a week. He had adopted this routine after a skirmish with the red coat army in a valley close to the Ravi.

Singh's mastery of *Kalaripayattu* had rendered the band of ten soldiers unconscious and immobile. It had been that very prowess that raised our suspicions and had made us scrutinise Mahendra Singh's face more closely. We began to recognise the unmistakable traces of Madhavan Nair in Mahendra Singh. His physical similarities to Madhavan Nair, the prowess in *Kalaripayattu* and an accidental utterance in Malayalam had been the giveaway. But at the same time, our conclusion was hindered by the memory of Madhavan Nair's body being fished out of the *Kulam* three years ago.

'So how did you confront him?' Charlotte asked, her curiosity had returned but her demeanour was more serious and reserved.

It had been the last day of our mission and the day before we embarked on our return to Calicut. Ten of the younger boys and Mahendra Singh would accompany the bullock bags on the barges while the rest of us would make our way by road. I had approached him to take his leave. 'Will I see you again, *Maashey*?' I asked hesitantly.

'*Maashey* means teacher doesn't it?' Charlotte asked and I nodded.

'How can a father stay away from his son for so long?' he said.

When he moved forward to hug me, he was still Mahendra Singh to me. When removed the turban to reveal his angular face, he transformed into Madhavan Nair, the man we had suspected him to be. But beyond that, my mind wasn't prepared to take any more leaps. The transition from Mahendra Singh to Madhavan Nair itself had been too fantastic.

I relived that moment again. He had looked at me with huge eyes that no longer seemed piercing or stern. Instead, they were full of abundant affection that washed away the many years of his absence in an instant.

As I narrated this, I noticed how Charlotte's eyes welled up and tears streamed down her face. She was happy for me. But I also knew how she longed for her Papa. I took Charlotte's hand, wiped her tears with my sleeve and held her as she sobbed on my shoulder. Feeling her head pressed against me, her warm tears moistening my shirt and her breath on my shoulder filled me with an overwhelming sense of affection and protectiveness for her.

Charlotte had gone to bed and Aaji and Sound had left as well. But Radha had remained.

'Aren't you tired, Radha? It is past midnight.' I said.

'I have seen the spirit.'

'What spirit, Radha?'

'The spirit of the Kulam, Chandran. It was she that led me to the forest.'

'What do you mean?'

'The butterfly, Chandran. She woke me. I followed her to the temple too and I coaxed Manikanthan.'

'Is that why your mother has been taking you the

vaidyan?'

'Yes. She thinks I have been sleepwalking so I've been forced to take those horrible medicines. I have been walking to the forest, then the temple and leading Manikanthan to the tunnels for several nights. I was guided by the spirit. I would return just before dawn, wash my feet at the well and then return to bed without anyone knowing. But *Amma* saw me washing my feet once and assumed I was sleepwalking in the *Tharavadu* grounds. I am awake at night so I am tired during the day. Charlotte has been upset because I don't go out anymore. But it is because I am so sleepy and tired. I can see the spirit. Chandran, you believe me, don't you? Is something wrong with me?'

'I believe you.'

'Can you see the spirit, Chandran?'

'Yes.'

'What does it mean? The spirits don't frighten me. Who are they?'

'She is the spirit of the Guardians.'

'The Guardians who protect Sita?'

'Yes.'

'Who else can see the spirits? The Zamorin?'

'Why do you ask that?'

'Because he was there.' 'There?'

'At the tunnels. He stood amidst fifty elephants, unafraid.

It was as though they all understood each other.'

This confirmed my hunch. It was who I suspected had led us from the beginning.

The cockerel announced the day of the *Ulsavam*. Some of us would remember each detail of the day: the side of the bed we had woken up on, the clothes we had chosen to wear, the breakfast we had eaten, the routine we had followed. And then we vowed we would never do the same again because of what had happened. Aaji, my best friend and my brother, was taken away from us that day.

Fort William, Calcutta, 1857

Fort William stood majestically on the banks of the Hooghly. It had been the muse of many artistes who had immortalised its ramparts in watercolours and oils. The horror of its interior had also been embedded in many minds. It was the ordeal and fatalities of the British prisoners captured by Siraj Ud Daulah's men in 1756 and their incarceration in a tiny cell (the Black Hole) that had precipitated the revenge of Clive and the War of Plassey in 1757.

A hundred years after the Battle of Plassey, dense clouds of dissent and unrest gathered in Bengal. The replacement of the Brown Bess musket with the new Enfields had caused disturbances amongst the Hindus and the Muslims. Northern India had erupted in violence. A patchwork blanket of land, brought together by the shrewd needlework of the East India Company, was alight with defiance and anger.

On route to the imposing Fort, Peter recollected his conversation with the colonel. There was talk of bringing back regiments from Russia, as well as the Gurkha soldiers from Nepal. 'The mutineers and the dissenters will be crushed,' the colonel had said.

Arriving at Fort William's gates, Peter shuddered at the thought of the plight of the prisoner housed in the cell only a floor below the Black Hole.

The guard was curt. 'Only twenty minutes.'

Shackled to a wooden chair, James looked weak. The chains seemed unnecessary. His skin was scored with scars, his bones jutted out and his hair was matted.

'If I had known you were coming, I would have scrubbed up better,' James said. Peter hugged James and blinked away the tears that pricked his eyes. They had known each other since childhood. They had been inseparable.

'Good to see you' Peter said, forcing a smile. He struggled with the burden he carried. He did not know how to break the news to James. He had been informed that morning by telegraph. An incident had occurred in Mallapuram, where the Zamorin had gone to broker peace between the feuding Namboothiris and Mopillas.

Prisoners at Fort William were not allowed visitors. When Peter joined the Bombay Presidency, his sole objective had been to achieve seniority that would help the cause. He also mentally prepared himself for the eventuality that it would allow benefits such as this one: A visit to an acquaintance serving a death sentence.

'How is he?' James' question stunned Peter. Had he deduced it from Peter's face? They were first cousins after all; James' mother and Peter's father were siblings. They were familiar with every expression and knew the workings of each other's minds better than they knew their own.

An attempt had been made on the Zamorin's life. He was clinging to life. The trembling of James' lips betrayed that he had heard the news.

'He will make it through. He is a fighter.'

'Who carried out the assassination attempt?' James asked in a quiet tone. The agitation on his face had been replaced by an expression Peter could not read.

'It was Chanakyan.'

'Arsenic?'

'Yes. The Zamorin had gone to Mallapuram to settle the dispute. The meeting between the Mopillas and the Namboothiris had been arranged at Manikyan Namboothiri's house. Chanakyan gained admission into the kitchen. Syed thinks the tea served at the gathering was spiked.'

The dispute between the Mopillas and the Namboothiris had started a century ago when a British Colonel had stripped the Namboothiri of a large portion of his ancestral lands and gifted it to the Mopillas to build a mosque. It had been the Zamorin's efforts over the last twenty years that kept the peace between the two feuding factions. However, something had triggered the communal strife once again and the Zamorin had been forced to mediate. It was for this that the Zamorin had travelled to Mallapuram.

'Peter, I know the Zamorin is critical. Chanakyan doesn't take chances. His doses are lethal.' James sounded stoic and seemed reconciled to the Zamorin's fate. He paused. 'How is Sarah?'

'You should have told her right at the start, James.' Peter regretted his tone immediately. His best friend and cousin was in a hopeless situation.

'I wish I had.' James had tears in his eyes. His head dropped onto the wooden table between them.

'You still can. Tell them both. They need to know the truth about you.' Peter stopped abruptly. He wanted to tell James about his conversation with Sarah but decided against it. He had hoped that Sarah would understand.

'Have you gone through Syed's drawings?' Peter asked, changing the topic.

'Yes. He has been meticulous. It is what I had suspected.

Have the boys managed to retrieve all of it?'

'Yes. The map was crucial. And it was you, James, who knew the significance of the pieces all along.' Peter said, feeling annoyed at his helplessness. He wished he could free his friend. The Guardians needed him. There was still so much to be done. If there was anyone who could put the Stele of Shu-Ilishu together, it was James. The final expedition to Sindh had been riddled with danger. But under Syed's leadership, Aaji, Chandran and the other boys had triumphed. Peter took out the scrapbook he had hidden inside his jacket.

Seeing the scrapbook, James' eyes momentarily lit up. 'Did Charlotte give this to you? How is she?' James asked, as he turned the pages of the scrapbook.

'No, I took it without asking. I thought you could use it to tell them your story,' he trailed off.

'In case I don't get out,' James said.

'Are they still torturing you?' Peter asked though he knew the answer to the question. James stayed silent.

'I brought you this.' He pushed a glass vial into James' hand. James looked at him and nodded.

'If it hadn't been for your warning, Syed and the boys would have been caught. We have been one step ahead of the Firm, thanks to your letters.'

James had infiltrated the Firm in Calcutta to give the Guardians a fighting chance. He knew that by rescuing Colin, he had drawn suspicion to himself. He was captured within a day. James would have preferred execution but he knew that it was too lenient a punishment for people who had betrayed the Firm. They would make him pay.

'The scrapbook will be ready for you,' James said.

He next day, Peter arrived at the Fort once again. The scrapbook was waiting for him but James wasn't. He had consumed the contents of the vial.

The cell was empty.

Outside the Fort, reinforcements from the Bombay Presidency and the Sikh regiments had arrived. The Meerut rebellion of 1857 would be crushed and hundreds would die.

6

A Family United

India, 1857

The Firm – Government House, Calcutta, May 1857

In the vast interior of the Government House—the palace Wellesley had made for himself in Calcutta—the front desk was dwarfed by the ocean of marble flooring. The desk itself had generous proportions and wore its walnut and ivory inlay with great dignity. Matheson presented himself at this desk and produced the card as instructed. He had received instructions in the post from the Governor.

He had never 'met' the Governor, not in the conventional sense of the word where parties sat face-to-face. Their 'meeting' had been fifteen years ago in surreal circumstances. He had only heard the Governor's voice on that occasion. It was as though the voice had travelled from the land of the living to his land of the dead. Matheson had since been resurrected by a medicine man.

All correspondence with the Governor since then had been through these visiting cards. On this occasion, he had instructed him to bring the trunk and present that card at the desk. The man at the desk had asked Matheson to proceed to the library.

Within the cavernous interiors of the House, he felt a surge of pride. He had never been inside a palace. The verandas swept on either side and the large marble urns stood like stout sentries. The men in the portraits looked at him. Queen Victoria sized him up through the elaborately carved mahogany frame.

'A surprise, lieutenant,' Matheson said when he saw the familiar face seated behind an ornate writing desk.

'Modest accommodation, isn't it?' the lieutenant asked as he gestured at the decorated walls and ceiling. The lieutenant didn't look remotely surprised to see Matheson, but he couldn't help but wonder why the lieutenant was here.

'Have you been here before?' the lieutenant continued.

'No,' Matheson replied as he felt the edges of the emblem of the card in his hand.

'Poseidon,' the lieutenant said.

'I don't understand,' Matheson said.

'It is the insignia on the card. Poseidon. He is the God of the Seas. Do you have the parcel?' the lieutenant asked. Matheson hesitated.

'I know about the parcel and the instruction for you to bring it here,' the lieutenant spoke in a quiet yet firm tone.

'I was asked to leave it at the desk. Shall I fetch it?' Matheson asked. The doubt in his mind lingered. What was it about the lieutenant's presence here that made him feel so self-conscious?

'No, that is not necessary. They will bring it up.' The lieutenant waited. He understood Matheson's hesitation. 'You have taken a look at its contents I presume? Did you wonder about the paintings?' the lieutenant asked.

'Yes. I shouldn't have, I am sorry.'

'No need to apologise, Matheson.'

'It has the painting that the judge kissed at your house that day!' Matheson attempted a chuckle to calm his fraught nerves. The Lieutenant did not respond and it heightened his awkwardness. He and the Lieutenant were friends. Why did he feel like an inexplicable wall of formality had crept up between them? Had the Governor invited the Lieutenant ? If yes then why hadn't the Lieutenant brought the paintings himself.

Two officers entered the room with the trunk between them. The Lieutenant gestured for the paintings to be removed.

'Tell me. Why were these paintings kept in a temple?' His eyes were focused on the paintings that were being laid out.

'The paintings have religious themes.' Matheson attempted, finding it impossible to shake the unexplainable diffidence.

'Will come back to that,' the Lieutenant said.

Matheson felt his heart slow down slightly. 'Any other reasons?'

'The artist is perhaps religious?' Matheson offered.

'EC could have religious importance. EC could be royal?' The lieutenant paced the room. 'I asked myself that

too. Is there a connection with the Zamorin? After all, he holds the trusteeship of the temple.'

'All the temple's precious artefacts are kept in the vaults.' Matheson volunteered.

'Yes, that is true. But not these paintings. These were kept in the inner sanctum in a place so sacred that no sane Indian would dare to trespass for fear of God's wrath. But we answer to no Gods.' The Lieutenant remembered the day his men had stolen the paintings on his orders. They had trooped into the sanctum while the priests had been preparing for the ceremony and the devotees distracted by the dancing elephant. The Lieutenant had asked his people to steal the deity's crown as a reward for their efforts.

'I felt sorry for the drunken judge. But I also have the fool to thank because if it weren't for him, I wouldn't have seen it.' the Lieutenant continued. 'It was what he saw. Not immediately visible to anyone of us that day but it was there all along, concealed by the clever EC.'

The Lieutenant stared at the painting of the gold deer that the inebriated judge had kissed that day at his mansion in Calicut.

'In the deer's pupils, I saw the face of a woman.'

'A woman?' Matheson asked.

'Yes. Just like how you see it if you look carefully at this other painting of a barren landscape. You see her blurred reflection in the shiny surface of the bow.' The Lieutenant gestured to the paintings one by one. 'Do you see her in the picture of the congregation?'

'Yes, I see her in the flames,' Matheson replied excitedly.

'Look carefully, Matheson. Do you see her in all three paintings?' the Lieutenant spoke, charged with emotion.

'Yes, I do. It is clever. Who is she?' Matheson asked. 'She is Sita,' the Lieutenant replied.

'From the *Ramayana?*' Matheson asked.

'Think about it. The golden deer and in its eyes, the woman; the scene in a king's court and a fire pit as her vague shadow walks through the flames; the field with a bow with her reflection. I didn't know the relevance of the bow until I read up on it. According to the *Ramayana,* Sita is said to have lifted a bow as a child. These are all episodes from the *Ramayana,* each one revolving around Sita, and are possibly deemed precious and sacred for that fact. It was why they were kept in a shrine.' The Lieutenant spoke with passion.

Matheson felt a sudden chill crawl up his spine. It was a sense of déjà vu as he was transported to the cold, damp interiors of a mud sarcophagus. His skin had tingled from the indescribable pain, his limbs immobile except for his fingers that scratched against the hard clay. There was an uneasy feeling in his eyes as he willed for his eyelids to open, only there were no eyelids and darkness was all around. It was the words of the Governor he had heard. Words through the clay walls of hell that reassured him that he was still alive. It was a voice that was unmistakable.

The lieutenant and the Governor were one and the same.

'EC, the Zamorin and even, if I may say, Sita, are all connected in some strange way. It is like a veil that hangs, covering a face of truth but just out of our grasp.' The Lieutenant paced the room.

'Say the word, Governor,' Matheson said the words slowly and deliberately. His eyes were peeled to the portion of the wall just behind the Governor's head, unable to bring his eyes to meet those of the man he would give his life for.

The Lieutenant looked at Matheson. The medicine man had excelled in the transplant. So many times he had been tempted to stare and marvel at the avian eyes but he had resisted. Now, he did so unobstructed. Part of him was elated that he had been able to keep his identity secret for so long from even one as shrewd as Matheson.

'I will finish Colin. I should have done so earlier.' Matheson said.

'Had you killed Colin, would we have found out where James' true loyalties lay?'

'Does Colin need to be kept alive?' Matheson asked.

'Not anymore. He has served his purpose. He led us to the wider group. He spoke about Aaji and Chandran's vermillion stained hands. He told us of Aaji's regular absences on a Thursday, the day he would assist at Chacko's father's tailoring shop. When we put Colin on his tail, Aaji changed his schedule. If there were nothing to hide about his day, would he have changed his schedule?'

Matheson nodded. His admiration for the Governor grew.

'I have Colin to thank for the shipping logs of the Carringham Shipping Company. Per the logs, calico and pepper have been shipped to London for many years.' The Governor looked at Matheson, waiting for a glimmer of recognition. He didn't disappoint.

'The company owned by the Earl of Saville, Lady Sarah's brother?' Matheson asked and the Governor gleamed.

'Though in recent times, the ships have been bringing drilling machines from Felixstowe to Calicut. Why? For years, the Carringham Company has done business with the Zamorin in pepper and calico. Then suddenly, drilling machines.' The Lieutenant paused.

'When all the shipping companies halted business in the subcontinent during the Vermillion Blight for fear of being sabotaged, the Carringham's shipping routes quadrupled. But here is the interesting part: The shipping route was between Karachi and Calicut.'

Matheson listened intently. His mind grew more and more restless. 'What can I do?'

'Sarah Carringham. But first, weaken the people of Calicut. They are loyal to their king. I will wind up operations here. The East India Company will not survive the revolt. I will meet you in Calicut.'

Colin

I had seen Chanakyan at the temple pavilion that evening.

We had congregated in high spirits. The Thali temple was the venue for the festival that the Zamorin and other trustees had been planning for years. Although the Zamorin's absence had been conspicuous, it had not impacted the festivities. Other temples from the neighbouring towns had joined in the celebration. The majestic elephants fidgeted in their finery. The mounted mahouts were tense with anxiety as they controlled the giants and waited for the percussionists to take their positions and lead the procession. The Thali temple drummers had been joined by their counterparts from the Padmanabhaswamy temple and the Thryambakeshwari temple. When the conch was blown, a steady beat resonated for miles. Little did we know that while the drumming was going on, Aaji was taking his last breath.

Krishnan Kutty had probably been shouting for a long time. But no one had heard him through the din of the percussion. But we knew something terrible had happened when he collapsed in front of the assembled elephants. He had discovered Aaji near the *naalamabalam*, slumped like a broken twig, battered and beaten and with a fatal gash on his head. There was blood everywhere. Sethuraman and Narayanan Kutty brought a blood-soaked Aaji to the entrance of the temple, hoping for a miracle. But it was too late.

I recalled Aaji's grin the day I had discovered his real name. I felt a deep pain in my chest when I realised that I wouldn't see that smile again. His death had been cruel and brutal. I found myself walking to where the gruesome event had taken place. A piece of dislodged granite lay on the spot, covered with blood. The grass beneath was flattened and smeared.

Beside it, there was a spot of damp, fresh red. It was not the muted hue of congealed blood but red of the masticated and disgusting *paan*. I knew at once who had done it. Chanakyan's presence at the temple had not been a coincidence.

In Calcutta, I had got a second chance. Dr. James had walked into Vidya Mandir, an oasis in the middle of Black Town. I owed him and Somesh my life.

'Enjoyed the sights and sounds of Black Town then?' he asked with a warm smile. I had been too stunned to respond. I hadn't expected to see him walk through the door.

'How did you know where to find me?' I asked.

'The people who sent you to Calcutta told me where to find you,' James answered.

'So they sent you to save me?' I asked.

'The Firm ordered me to kill you, Colin,' James replied, expressionless.

'What Firm? I don't work for any Firm.' I said emphatically. 'Danny, I won't hurt you.'

I looked at James. He knew my real name?

'Let me tell you my story, Danny.' That name again.

How did he know?

'I was appointed surgeon to the Zamorin. That is no secret to you.' he said. He looked at me like an equal, not like he was worth ten of me or like he was the affluent brother-in-law of the wealthiest Earl in England.

'It is lucky that the Zamorin didn't have any major affliction as it might have soon become obvious that I wasn't much of a doctor to him. I was too busy making myself known to the senior officials of the Company and indispensable to the merchants and bishops who were trooping into the country. I notched a long list of impressive contacts. My social calendar boasted of hunting trips with the Maharajas of Jodhpur, holidays in Ooty with the Nizam's entourage and vacations with the Maharaja Wodeyar of Mysore.'

I looked at him. James' tone wasn't bombastic. But his words painted a picture of grandeur and fame.

'And then I was invited to join the Firm. I had reached the summit. The ruse had worked but this would be the acid test. It was what I dreaded the most. It was not my dream to get into the Firm. But I had to get in to protect a dream. I had to become one of them. Every day, I battled with the fear of being found out. You must know the feeling?'

I froze. He knew my secret—my identity. The tightness crept back in.

'I infiltrated their establishment to protect my people. What people, you ask? I see the question in your eyes. I am part of a group that wants to preserve our past. Without the legacy of our forefathers, past lessons will be forgotten. The Firm was close to finding it. They wanted to plunder the relics of a great civilisation.'

His words made no sense. Why was he telling me all this? My head hurt and I was unable to concentrate. What was this civilisation?

'The East India Company was moving fast with their plans for the railways. If their Lahore and Multan line were to go ahead, the relics would be destroyed during the preparation and construction of the line. Danny, our civilisation's legacy is buried across the plains of the north.' He paused. My eyes couldn't focus. My head was a blur.

'We had to act fast. But with the Firm close at our heels, we needed to stay one step ahead. It was why I infiltrated them. It took us some time to understand the methods of the Firm. There was a pattern: liquidation of assets, sudden transfers to and from key posts in the army and civil services, recruitment of local thugs, the formation of a historical society to veil an illegal black market operation.'

James paused. 'Like the Calicut Chapter of the Asiatic Society.'

The constriction in my chest deepened. My head throbbed. 'Captain Matheson and Chanakyan are all a part of this Firm?' I asked.

'Yes, them and their leader, the Governor.'

There was a sudden moment of clarity. James' words had pierced through the stupor. I remembered a story the lieutenant had told me. It was of his near escape from death. He had taken charge of a clandestine mission—a cargo of Egyptian artefacts that had to be relocated at the behest of the Church in Rome and the British government.

It was rumoured that the symbols on the relics, when translated, had revealed that they belonged to the period that coincided with that of the cataclysmic floods—an event which, according to the Bible, had destroyed all life. The existence of the relics had brought the teachings of the Bible into question. To avoid controversy, the authorities had decided to hide the artefacts until a more appropriate time.

However, the ship had capsized in a storm and the treasures were lost at sea. But the lieutenant had miraculously managed to survive by the skin of his teeth. When he had narrated this I had marvelled at his heroism. But had the ship capsized at all? The lieutenant could still have in his possession a cargo load of controversial relics that, by virtue of its nature, would be infinitely more valuable.

The fog had lifted. I had been a fool. The Governor of the Firm was none other than the lieutenant. I was in no doubt. James watched me and nodded. It was as though he read my mind. I had been a pawn in the sinister operations of the Firm. I had even spied on Aaji. The image of my mother and my brother floated in front of my eyes. Guilt gripped me.

'Why are you telling me all this? How do you know you can trust me?' I asked feebly.

'That is because you have been vetted. You trusted someone with your observations and your problems. Our Kutty Ettan, or who you know as N Kutty, knew the real you—the Danny MacFayden hidden beneath Colin Coquettish.' James said with a reassuring smile.

'It was he who recruited you to our cause. Every time you confided in him, you were giving us information. Had it not been for you, we would have never known the intricate details of the Company's Railway plans. Without you, it would have been impossible to confirm our suspicions on the double identity of the lieutenant, Jim Burtenshaw, Governor of the Firm.'

It was the first time I had heard his name. I had seen initials JB on some of his books. But it had never seemed of consequence. He was the lieutenant to me. I had even thought of him as a godfather, which now made me feel sick.

'Don't go back to Calicut Danny. You should return to Ireland. Somesh can help you with the arrangements.'

Sitting with James and Somesh, I suddenly felt as though I belonged. I didn't have to pretend. I felt a pang of longing. I missed the Kutumbam. I missed Carly.

'So what happens next?' Inside, I knew the answer to my question. I felt a surge of overwhelming guilt. James had blown his cover to save my life. The Firm wouldn't spare him.

'Well, the Firm won't have me. So perhaps go back to good old fashioned medicine.' James said cheerfully.

I returned to Calicut despite James' instruction. I was fired with zeal to be of service to the *Tharavadu* household. The four walls housed members of a noble lineage. Narayanan Kutty was just one of whom had been named. It didn't take a great deal of intelligence to work out that every one of them was a part of it. When I returned to the *Tharavadu*, it welcomed me with open arms. I felt as if I had come home. But I couldn't meet Lady Sarah's eyes. I couldn't bring myself to tell her that her husband was probably dead by now and that it was all because of me. Aaji's death spurred me to finish Chanakyan, Matheson and Jim Burtenshaw. Or die trying.

Aaji's death was used to fuel a communal rift. The Namboothiris and the Mopillas had been at daggers for a while and when the local police station announced that they suspected a Hindu group behind Aaji's death, all hell broke loose. The Firm was behind it. Only they were capable of such evil. Aaji was a Muslim boy raised by the priests at the temple and then adopted by Krishnan Kutty's Hindu family. Really, there couldn't have been a better example of communal unity. But his death was now being used to create communal discord.

Temples and homes were ransacked by Captain Matheson and his men. In preparation, Narayanan Kutty had organised for a rotating group of armed men outside the *Maradu Tharavadu*. Soujanya and Chandran took shifts along with Sethuraman. The Kuruchiyar tribals moved into the forests behind the Maradu to provide protection. The house was being fortified from all sides.

There was nothing exceptional about the sunrise on the morning of 30th June 1857. There was nothing about that morning that suggested the exceptional events of the day to come. Men, women, children and even some sepoys had gathered for the peaceful protest. We knew that Matheson's men would arrive at our home soon. I would do all I could to protect it. But there was something I needed to do first.

I was told I would find them on the beach. Narayanan Kutty had escorted Carly and Charlotte. They were going to set sail for England. Carly looked beautiful in a simple, off-white calico dress. Narayanan Kutty looked at me and smiled. He took Charlotte aside. Carly smiled cheerfully, her lips twitching and her chin wrinkled.

'Have you ever been to Ireland, Carly?'

'No.'

'Would you like to go?'

'Of course. I am expecting a proper grand wedding at the Sophia church at Cork in front of all those drunken Irish relatives of yours. Don't think I am going to be happy with simply exchanging jasmine garlands in front of the Goddess Sita in a ceremony officiated by N Cutie. No offence Cutie.'

'None taken, Carly Madam.' Narayanan Kutty blushed. Carly had been addressing him as Cutie for five years and he still couldn't refrain from breaking into his idiotic smile.

She had spoken quickly, hiding her emotion with her mock angry tone. It made my heart ache knowing that I would probably not see her again. 'You could open a bakery in Cork, Carly.'

Carly smiled as tears streamed down her face. 'A spring wedding and a bakery. We will have a girl and a boy. I will call them Kutty and Kutty.'

I bid Charlotte and Carly goodbye and made my way to Kuttuchira Road, where I waited. The chaos and the noise had been replaced with a death-like silence. With the unrest in the north of India, the officers in Calicut were taking no chances. A curfew had been imposed.

'Thank you for meeting me here, Colin.' Lady Sarah smiled feebly. She had come as promised. 'Did James look well when you saw him last?'

I nodded.

She didn't ask anything more. She was being very strong. 'Did you bid Carly farewell?'

I nodded.

'You shouldn't come with me, Colin. This is my battle.'

I nodded and took the tiny vial of arsenic from her. 'It's my battle too,' I muttered under my breath. Together, we made our way to the lieutenant's house.

—⇒⟫⟪⇐—

Colin opened the cupboard only to be greeted by an old friend, the lumper plant. It wasn't the sheer size of it that transfixed him. It was the embrace as the stem coiled around him and pulled him towards it. Its tendrils and leaves tickled his ears. The blooms were plenty. He shut his eyes and he could see his mother and brother's faces. This time, they looked happy and well fed. Their eyes brimmed with tears of happiness. He felt a warm surge of redemption, not the burrowing hole in the pit of his chest that he had felt ever since he left Ireland. Here, so many thousands of miles away from his homeland, he had found purpose. It didn't matter who he was fighting. What mattered were his principles. Here, he would get his chance to be redeemed.

—⇒⟫⟪⇐—

Charlotte

'Carly, did you know that the Malayalam word for grandfather is *acchachan*?' I asked her while we waited on the beach for the ship that would take us back to England.

I had learnt the identity of my grandfather the day before and I was to leave without saying a proper goodbye. It had been Mama who insisted we leave for England immediately. I wanted to stay but she had been adamant. My pleas had no affect on her.

Carly and I sat on the beach, drawing pictures of coconut trees and the profile of our beloved *Maradu* house on the sand. At a distance, I could see a ship on the horizon—the ship that would take us away from all of this.

Carly looked at me affectionately. 'Don't have any regrets, Charlotte. If you want to say goodbye to your *acchachan*, go do it now.' I hugged her and wept. She held me tight and didn't want to let go. Perhaps she knew.

Narayanan Kutty had been waiting to make sure that we got onto the ship. As I turned around and walked towards the town, he tried to stop me. But Carly intervened.

I had misunderstood him. N Kutty had been our protector all along. Even today, in the midst of the unrest, he had been loyal, escorting us to make sure we were safe.

The first protest march had been held at SM Street a few days after Aaji's death. A *mullah* took his position a few yards away from our gatehouse. He was accompanied by a group of senior Mopillas, who sat down in the middle of the street.

S.M. Street had doffed its hat of noisiness in respect. Twenty individuals bearing *mridangams* started a steady beat. They led a group of musicians who played the melancholy strains of the *naadasuram* and a group of priests from the temples chanted briefly. Disciples of Thyagaraja had travelled from Thanjavur to participate in the event. Their songs resonated with patriotic zeal. Some joined the singing while others clapped their hands. '*Jai Bharatham, Jai Bharatham, Jai Bharatham,*' reverberated across the street.

Mr. C had carried his flute in the pocket of his trousers for years. It was the one luxury he allowed himself—a reminder of his family and days in his native Cork. He was momentarily stunned by the reflex that had made him whip it out and play its haunting melody. The crowds had been stunned too. There was no stopping them. A Sahib had joined them. It was how the musical protest in Calicut began.

At first, the Company dismissed our musical movement as silly. But when some sepoys joined the movement and the natives grew in confidence, the top brass got nervous. The uprising in Meerut, Awadh and parts of Bengal had prepared them. They weren't going to take any chances. And so they came with reinforcements.

So much had changed in such a short span of time. We had all changed. The drumming in my head had become a permanent fixture. The sight of Aaji's father stumbling between the drummers, holding his blood-smeared hands aloft still haunted me. It was that scene that woke me at night. I was scared and frightened for all of us. Suddenly, life had become so threatening.

Radha would hover around Chandran, watching his every move, sitting by his side at meal times and even by his bedside when he went to sleep. She had lost her brother. She was determined to not lose Chandran. Chandran couldn't bear it. He had become quiet and grim, almost unrecognisable. He didn't speak to me and avoided my company. Sound had taken charge of Radha. He followed her with a plate of food or glass of milk, ensuring she ate or drank something. He was devoted to her.

More than the hurt and the anguish, it was guilt that suffocated me. I knew I had been responsible for Aaji's death. I knew that the letter I had shown him had troubled him. It was the letter that had sent Aaji in pursuit of Chanakyan.

It was on the night after we rejoiced in Chandran and Aaji's return from Sindh. When Chandran had spoken of the Scind Dawk postage stamp and letters, I knew that the stamps Papa had brought to my attention all those months ago were important. I had shown the letters to Aaji and he examined them with great care.

One, he had said, was a blank letter with a pristine stamp. The other had cancellation marks along with the intentional indents of the cypher. It was fascinating. The marks of the cypher were only obvious to a person with a trained eye. Aaji had used a piece of paper to decode the cryptic message in the letter.

Dear James,

Chanakyan and Matheson killed Chacko. Have you met Syed as yet?

My regards to your father.

Best wishes PC.

This letter had uncovered a side of Papa I hadn't known. Papa had known of Syed. It was then that it occurred to me that it was Papa who declared Madhavan Nair dead after the incident at the *Kulam*. Could he have known that Madhavan Nair was Syed, Chandran's father, all along? Was it Papa's expertise with concoctions that enabled them to fake Madhavan Nair's death?

I read the penultimate line several times. 'Regards to your father,' it said. But Papa's father was dead. Or so I thought. Why had Papa hidden this from us?

At the time, I had been so preoccupied with the implications of the letter that I had completely ignored how serious Aaji had become and did not pay attention to his long absences from the house. But now, as I watched his devastated family, I felt torn with guilt. I had to tell someone. So when I saw Chandran in the courtyard, I approached him.

Chandran looked away and I couldn't bear it. I deserved it. If I hadn't shown Aaji the letter, he would still be alive. I ran into the grove, sobbing uncontrollably. But Chandran followed. He held my hand and took me to the jackfruit tree on whose trunk he had etched my name. I felt even more ashamed and undeserving of his affection. I sobbed loudly. He apologised for offending me and I cried harder. My words were too garbled for him to understand. Chandran waited patiently for me to calm down.

'I am to blame for Aaji's death,' I finally managed to say to him. I showed him the letter and the paper in which Aaji had scribbled the message. I realised this was the only note Aaji had written to me and hence the most precious thing I possessed.

Chandran's face darkened. 'Chanakyan,' he muttered softly, his jaw tightening. 'It's not your fault, Charlotte. You had nothing to do with this. Please don't blame yourself. You should show the letter to your mother. She needs to know the truth about your Papa.' I stared at him but Chandran held my hand and managed a small smile. 'PC is Peter Charleston. Your Papa and Captain Charleston have been the backbone of our operation.'

Mama stared at the message Aaji had scribbled. I watched as the expression on her face changed. Her eyes were glazed, as though she were a million miles away. She didn't utter a word. Finally, she got up, saying that she needed to meet the Zamorin. She had been gone for a few hours but returned just after the evening prayers at the Thali temple. She seemed transformed, her face unflinching like granite.

'I have something to show you, Charlotte,' she said. She took my hand and led me to Papa's armchair. It remained in the same place he had left it. I wished he were here, sitting on the chair, his eyes glued to the door that led to the *Kulam*. N Kutty was standing at the door. He smiled at me. It was only when N Kutty removed the picture from above the door and placed it on the stool next to us that I noticed the face in the painting. It was a faded miniature portrait of a European woman, overshadowed by the bulky frame that surrounded the picture.

'This is Emily Charleston, the artist who created the mural in your room. I will tell you about her. But N Kutty wants to show us something first.' Mama said.

N Kutty turned the knob at the centre of the ornate *Kulam* door. Then he repeated the manoeuvre on eleven other knobs arranged across the door. We heard a loud thud and felt the floor vibrate under our feet.

N Kutty then crouched on the step in front of the *Kulam* door and gave it a sideways push. Unexpectedly, the step moved and revealed a cavity in the floor. 'This,' he said helpfully, 'leads to a chamber under the *Kulam*. It is where we have hidden the precious cargo from Sindh.'

As though reading my mind, N Kutty gestured for me to follow him. We slid down into the cavity and landed on the soft ground a few feet beneath us. The ceiling was only a few inches higher than N Kutty. In front of us, there was a wall suspended from the roof, barely hovering a couple of feet above the ground.

N Kutty explained that it was pulled up by the screws he had turned on the door. He crept beneath the wall and we entered a chamber that seemed to be carved into the rock. This was much darker and I could barely make out his silhouette in front of me. A strange lapping sound echoed through the chamber. 'It is the water in the *Kulam* above you,' he said.

I could just make out a pile of bags arranged neatly along the wall. He explained it was made of bullock skin and had been commonly used in the North-West of India. 'Some of the smaller articles were shipped in these,' he said. 'This is only one of many, many underground cellars. The tunnels stretch for many kilometres. There is one that runs under the Mananchira Tank and the Dutch factory.'

The lantern that Narayanan Kutty carried started to flicker and we made our way back. Mama was waiting for us anxiously and I described what I had seen. The entire episode was strangely familiar like I had experienced it before. And then I realised. I turned to Mama. 'That mural in my room, it depicts these chambers under the *Kulam*. It is so clever! N Kutty says there are many miles of tunnels underneath!'

He smiled.

'That brings me to the artist of the mural and the lady in the portrait,' Mama said.

'Emily Charleston and the Zamorin are your Papa's parents. They are your grandparents...'

That night, we dined with the Zamorin, my grandfather. My grandfather didn't eat. He was too weak. In different circumstances, the dinner would have been a joyous occasion. Mama had told me that Papa was imprisoned in Calcutta. Although she spoke with equanimity, I sensed from her expression and the general mood of the house that there was something more sinister afoot. Mama told me that she had decided to send me to England with Carly the next day. I could do nothing to change her mind. I said goodbye to everyone in the Tharavadu except Chandran. I couldn't bring myself to say goodbye to the boy I loved.

A s N Kutty and I walked back from the beach, I thought of how I would say goodbye to my grandfather. I wanted to tell him how happy I was to be his grandchild. We approached the grand gatehouse of the palace. There was a roar of thunder and the heavens opened. There was a crowd of people who had gathered at the *Padmini Vilasam*, ignoring the curfew. N Kutty took my hand in his and clutched it hard.

I looked at him and saw his jaw tighten, his cheeks taut as he fought the tears that stung his eyes. I prepared myself for the news. It was unfair. I hadn't called him *acchachan* enough times. I knew him as my grandfather for only a day. But I consoled myself with the thought that even though I had been ignorant of the blood relationship we shared, I admired him, respected him and adored him. That would never change.

Sethuraman emerged from the crowd. 'The Zamorin died an hour ago, Chiri Kutty,' he said.

My *acchachan* had died. I hadn't had the chance to say goodbye. My grandfather and my friend Aaji had been taken from me in the span of two weeks. I would go back to the *Tharavadu*, despite my mother's orders. This was my family. The *Maradu* was my home. I would go back there even if it were the last thing I did.

Sarah

The Kuruchiyar tribals had descended on the forest at the back of the *Tharavadu* as a mark of solidarity. Narayanan Kutty, Chandran and Soujanya took turns to guard the entrance. Narayanan Kutty was a leader, resolute and firm in his decisions and almost cold and detached to all that had transpired. Fear and dread spread through the house and we felt vulnerable. As if all this wretchedness weren't enough, a threat of even sinister events was looming outside.

A week before Aaji had been murdered, an attempt had been made on the Zamorin's life. It had been Narayanan Kutty who confided to me the truth. The attempt on his life had been kept a secret. The people of Calicut needed a leader at this time of crisis and news of an assassination attempt would only unleash terror and chaos on an uneasy people.

Chanakyan had disappeared after the assassination attempt. A frail body had been made even more fragile. The Zamorin stopped eating. But a combination of his iron resolve and herbal medication stabilised him. After Aaji's murder, two of the Zamorin's closest aides had been arrested. Tenant farmers loyal to the Zamorin had been arrested too without a warrant. There were malicious forces at work, seeking to weaken the Zamorin.

The letter that Charlotte showed me was an indication that Peter and James had been involved in the Cause. The

'*Ettan*' or older brother that Aaji, Chandran and Sethuraman had referred to on many occasions before had been a genius of planning: someone who had managed to fake the death of Madhavan Nair so convincingly; someone who had created the drugs that had knocked the guards unconscious at the indigo depot; someone with a medical background and access to British medicines that mysteriously found their way to the Thali temple to treat the sick hordes. The churning in my mind stopped and the image of one person solidified, just as an ugly mass of doubt and suspicion began to dissolve.

Could it be that James and I had been on the same side all along? But who was that woman with him at the Club? I tried to recall every detail of our voyage to India and the months before, trying to cling to the memories of those beautiful moments together, back when we had been so close.

As I examined our conversations, it became clear to me that James had been preparing for his role in India all along.

His extensive knowledge of India's and Britain's past, his long and arduous penance in his library and office and his hair and clothes often smelling of the formulations he had been researching had all been in preparation for the role he would play. Peter's words, 'James has a family', ran in an endless loop through my head.

I knew the Zamorin would have the answers.

'I am glad you have come, Sarah.' The Zamorin was lying down when I went to see him. He looked smaller than before. Even the soft *mundu* seemed like a tremendous load on his emaciated body. He gestured for me to sit.

'Your shoes are hurting you?' he asked, gesturing at my feet. Even in his condition, he noticed that my limp had worsened. It was my fault. I shouldn't have hurried the way I had. My mind had been reeling with numerous thoughts and questions.

'You had a brush with death when you were sixteen, Saaru.' I nodded as though I were in a trance. He continued. 'Your constitution is feeble but you show compassion in every small action. That day in the temple, you came face-to-face with a scale of tragedy you had not witnessed before. You allowed the shock and the grief to overwhelm you. But your service at the Thali temple from that day on has been an inspiration to many. Caste and class did not make any difference to you. You sat on the ground, amidst the filth and disease, without hesitation. Your inability to speak Malayalam didn't stop you from showing your care and concern. To the many who came from the dark and dirty slums of Calicut and accepted their dreadful fate of disease and deprivation, your words and your care was heaven.'

My eyes stung with tears.

'I have to apologise. It was because of me James didn't tell you everything. I am to blame. I thought I was protecting you and Chiri. James has been in Calcutta all this time, working for our cause. He has been in pursuit of Jim Burtenshaw and his uncle, Joshua Burtenshaw, the opium tycoon, the very man who deceived and cheated your grandfather of all his wealth.'

I sat silent, allowing his words to sink in.

'There is something I want to show you,' he said feebly. He called out to Syed who was standing guard outside his room. Syed opened the shutters and the light poured in. It was a warm and humid day. I turned to look at the Zamorin and saw that though his face was the colour of ash, a smile played on his lips. The birds chirruped incessantly. I cleared my throat to speak but he lifted his hand and silenced me. I had many questions. But I knew they would have to wait. The shutter suddenly closed, cloaking us in semi-darkness. I was startled but the Zamorin seemed to have been expecting it.

'It is dusk now. The evening prayers in the Thali temple must have concluded. Do you know what my favourite part of the *deeparadhana* is? It is the *prasadam*; the fragrance of the *thetchi* flowers and the smell of the freshly grounded sandalwood paste in rosewater. Aaji knew that.' He faltered slightly and his chin trembled.

The Zamorin gestured to Syed to open the shutter again. The light streamed in along with an intoxicating smell of sandalwood. Hanging from the bar of the window was a garland of *thetchi* flowers and the banana-leaf parcel of sandalwood and ash. Syed placed them in the Zamorin's outstretched hands.

'Aaji has not forgotten,' the Zamorin said as he applied the paste on his forehead and neck. Syed explained that for weeks, the Zamorin had been unable to attend the *deeparadhana*. But Aaji had brought him the *prasadam* from the temple every evening and placed it in the same spot. It had been days since Aaji had died but the ritual continued. The *thetchi* and the sandalwood paste still made it to the Zamorin's windowsill.

'But Aaji is dead. What does this mean? Who is bringing this for you?' I asked. 'It can't be Aaji?'

'You have seen the blue butterfly, haven't you?' the Zamorin asked, not answering my question. 'You are wondering how I know. James used to see her too. She liked to flutter in her favourite place, the *Kulam*. You saw her hovering there too, didn't you?' he asked softly.

'Who is she- the butterfly? '

'She is Emily. My beloved wife. It is her spirit that lives in the blue butterfly of the *Kulam*. Her spirit lives on, just as Aaji's spirit does. It is Aaji's spirit that brings me the *prasadam* from the temple.' The Zamorin paused then continued in a low tone. 'Emily Charleston is the mother of James and his sister, Revathy. It was Revathy you saw at the Club with him.'

It was as though someone had pushed me into an ice-cold lake. James was the Zamorin's son. The idea bobbed in my head but refused to sink in. Peter's words came back to me. 'James has a family here.' The exotic woman with James was his sister, Revathy.

My legs trembled. My eyes prickled. My throat was parched. I felt horrid for the aspersions I had cast on my husband. I longed to see James. The man I had married had grown in stature in my eyes. James wasn't just a doctor. He was also a passionate and noble man, just like his father. The physical appearance of the siblings had concealed their noble lineage. Their olive skin tone and their light eyes had given them an alluring quality. But I didn't dream that their features had been the product of a marriage between two different cultures and races.

'The Guardians don't die,' the Zamorin said. 'Chacko, Aaji, my Emily and James paid with their lives as they carried out their noble tasks.' He paused as I collapsed to the floor, still clutching his bony hand.

James was gone. The realisation that I had lost my husband cut through my being like a knife.

'Saaru, their bodies have perished. But the Universe conspires to keep their spirits alive. The spirit of the Guardians live on. The *Maradu Tharavadu* is much more than a house.

It leads to the Goddess. Promise me you will not let the Firm find her.'

--➤➤◄◄--

'For too many years we have meddled. This has gone too far. Trees, animals and plants perish.'

'What will you do?'

'I will end it once and for all.'

'You can't end it without destroying it all.'

'Then so be it.'

'This was the cataclysm you saw in the vision.'

'Yes.'

'You can't do this alone.'

'With Saraswathy by my side, I have nothing to fear. The next rains will be heavier than usual. The river Goddess will surge down with tenfold her power.'

'But what if she cannot wash away the poison?'

'It will burn first.'

'Burn?'

'Yes. The monkey people will help.'

'They believe it must be done. Their leader will torch every living thing with his tail.'

'Everything will be incinerated.'

'It must be done. Otherwise, there is no future.'
'Dear Seer, you know you will perish.'

'It is a small price to pay.'

--➤➤◄◄--

Calicut, India, July 1857

In the aftermath of the violence, the lobby of the hospital had become a makeshift office. Police constables and people argued and shouted. Officers scrolled through lists of missing people. Snippets of conversation deposited on Peter's ears.

'The hoodlums bound Lieutenant Burtenshaw. Two young men and a lady were involved. But there's no confirmation of their identities. Burtenshaw is dead. He was poisoned.'

In the corner, he recognised the group of Mopillas. 'The Zamorin's body has vanished.'

'The *Maradu* house was destroyed in the fire.'

The words ricocheted in Peter's head like fireworks. His eyes twitched, his mouth was dry and a burning raged within him. His hands were clenched so tight his nails pierced through the flesh of his palms. Peter looked at the list of missing persons. Amongst the sea of people that had gathered in the lobby, Peter saw Somesh. His chubby face looked grey. His eyes had a crescent of darkness under them.

Somesh took Peter by his arm and led him away. 'There is something you have to see,' he said.

They went to the *Maradu Tharavadu* and stood outside the gatehouse. It looked untouched as if the violent events of yesterday were just fiction. Peter refused to enter. 'I don't want to go in.'

'You must.'

There was no house, just the remains of a horrific bonfire. Bodies were strewn across the ground—some twisted and mangled.

'See over there. Matheson's body lies with the musket. He shot Charlotte five times. Narayanan Kutty walked into his musket. He killed Matheson before he succumbed. There was a loud explosion after that. The *Tharavadu* became dust.'

Peter felt a ringing in his ears. The sounds of bullets and shrieks. He was not a stranger to war. But this had been an unequal and unfair battle.

'But their bodies are not here.'

Peter looked at Somesh confused. 'What are you saying, Somesh? The bodies are here. Look around you.'

'Charlotte's and Narayanan Kutty's bodies are not. Her Ladyships' is not. No one from the Maradu house is here.'

Peter looked around. It was true. Their bodies were not there. All that remained of the beloved house were its crumbs and splinters of wood. The mangled corpses of the goons were strewn around but there was not a trace of the remains of the *Maradu* household. Despite the explosion, there should have been traces of its residents—bones, clothes, something.

'Somesh, how did you know? How did you know that Charlotte was shot five times and that Narayanan Kutty killed Matheson?'

'We were here.'

'We who?'

'James and I.'

7

Interlude

Travancore, July 1857

Revathy's labour was brought on by a thundering clap. It was the deafening sound of the Kilimanoor Palace doors being smashed open. An unnerving silence followed the commotion and Princess Revathy knew that the hyenas prowled through her sanctuary. Thousands of years of positive culture graced the walls in the form of exquisite handicraft and finely honed skill, but through those corridors traversed a savage people, ready to tear it to shreds. Once upon a time, these soldiers had fought alongside her father and her husband. But now, they had sold their souls to the Firm.

Paralysed by contractions, she could barely move. It had come early. Too early. She prayed it was only momentary and willed for them to stop. Her baby needed more time. At first, she thought she had imagined them. Shock and grief can do that to a body. Her father murdered, her brother imprisoned and her sister-in-law trapped in a doomed battle.

The pain in her heart had radiated through her, grasping and ebbing in rhythm. She forced her mind to chant.

On occasions in the past, it had helped focus her mind, preparing her body for the rigour of *Kalaripayattu*. But here, the chant had no effect. Her mind thrashed about like a fish out of water. The contractions were real and were not a manifestation of bereavement.

Her room, located deep within the palace, was only a few feet away from the threatening footsteps of the mercenaries. But her friend's face, luminous and reassuring like the moon, had given her solace in the grim howling darkness.

'You will survive this, Revathy,' her friend said as she held her hand.

She was distracted by a soft knocking. It came from the large rosewood cupboard in her room. Her friend calmly walked towards it. Outside her room, Revathy could hear the scraping and ominous whispers of the predators. They were close now. Her friend was next to her, whispering words of comfort. But she couldn't hear them. A numbing pain coiled around her body. A searing pain shot through her belly and the sound of whispers and the crashing of bullets against her bedroom door deafened her.

The dark interiors of her cupboard engulfed her. She saw the faces of two men she didn't recognise. She couldn't bring herself to look at their eyes. Was this the end? She felt a warmth on her upper arm. A soft palm held her as she felt herself being lifted. 'There is a tunnel, Revathy. It will be difficult but I will help you.' Again darkness. This time, it embraced her as she went into a long sleep.

She woke up, her lips dry and her body throbbing with pain. She was inside a cart. It shuddered, jostling at a terrific pace. The fists of the wind pummelled its walls. She felt a cold, damp mass against her chest. Her eyes found a head matted with blood. She closed her eyes and opened them again. Her arms hugged the baby, willing it to breathe while her entire body sobbed.

'Please come back to me. I cannot lose you too.'

Again darkness as she yielded to the pain and fatigue.

T he hut stood with gumption within the thick forest of the Nilgiris. In the sodden calico saree, with her hair matted and stuck to her scalp, she held the quivering body of the one-day-old baby. She was still but there was life pulsating through hers veins. She laughed at the irony of fate. Everyone else had been taken. Only she and her one-day-old fragile daughter were left.

Her friend sat beside her. She took the princess's hand as she had done the day she arrived at the palace's doorstep.

'My brother sent you?' Revathy had asked. 'No, Sarah did,' the companion had told her.

'Sarah's need is more.' Revathy's thoughts didn't materialise into words. She knew the mountain of responsibility on Sarah's shoulders. She corrected herself. It was not a mountain. It was the path of duty her sister-in-law had chosen. Or had duty chosen her? Lying here under the influence of the medicine, she found her thoughts extraordinarily lucid.

'Great responsibility is akin to a mountain, some find it unsurmountable and then there are others like Hanuman whose whole hearted gumption and abundant spirit can lift mountains on their finger – tips.'

There was a whimper. Revathy tried to lift herself but she found the effort excruciating. Her friend lifted her daughter and rocked her, humming a familiar lullaby. She could see her pink chapped skin smoothed by her bronze hands; she could make out her tentative breathing become stronger and more rhythmic with her gentle caress.

She was two months too early into this world and yet in the hands of this doting nurse, she gained vigour with every passing minute. Outside, the sun had shoved the clouds aside. The rain clouds moved reluctantly. In life's drama, they were star performers. Her role and her daughter's role in this unfolding and evolving saga of millennia was miniscule. The events of the last few days had distracted her from what was really important: that she and her daughter had made it against all odds.

She felt her eyes drawn to her companion, who was the personification of serenity. The latter traced Revathy's lifeline on her palm. The line lifted; Revathy's eyes followed it, hypnotised. The line blurred. As she felt her tear glands swell up, she found the line fill with water. It snaked around her and the baby. It meandered like a river. She saw houses spring from its banks and then people she didn't recognise.

Slowly, the landscape changed. The land enveloped in a haze. In that smoke, she saw his stoic face. Revathy recognised the seer of Meluhha immediately. The unfolding scenes made her heart beat quicker. She knew what was coming. This was a story she knew well: A bustling village and the man who sat on the bank, unphased by the raging inferno that hurled at him.

The villages burned. But the lifeline had transformed. Frothing and bubbling, the river now was a churning ocean. The burning inferno was a small pellet compared to the awesome majesty of the river. The inferno succumbed and all was quiet.

Revathy looked at her friend. The bronze of her skin glistened as the sun outside prepared for its descent. Her eyes shone—her pupils glowed, its blue pattern arresting. Revathy watched as her friend lifted her arms and then dropped them gently to her lap.

The river obeyed; it mellowed. It descended into Revathy's palm. She felt its tingling cold on her skin. It extended through her wrist into the hand of her baby, from one generation to the next. The river Goddess had seen so many generations. Revathy and her baby, her father, her brother, James, and Sarah were only pebbles in its extraordinary journey.

She looked at her companion with reverence.

'It cannot be finished. Not when it has barely started.'

Her friend didn't say anything. Instead, she turned and opened the door. The breeze tumbled in, bringing with it its finds. A terrapin slowly ambled into the hut. Revathy gasped. 'Hercules!' she exclaimed. Its mountain-like shell was too tall and wide for the door. The walls dissolved momentarily, so the majestic creature could enter. It crouched at the edge of the cot.

A giant vulture flew in and nestled on the rafters above. Its wing bore the pattern of a slash. The branch of the ancient Sanjeevini plant outstretched its hands and caressed the baby's cheek. Yellow petals of the *champakam* fell at their feet. There was a screeching of birds in the distance. A long metallic snout pushed through the entrance, its scales shimmering in the sun and its spiky tail swished delicately into the side, coming to rest beside the terrapin. They had shared the waters thousands of years ago and here they were again. The baby's hand rubbed the scaly head of the alligator, who rested after his long journey across seas and oceans. Outside, a crowd of white-bodied and black-faced monkeys gathered in their hundreds with fruits for the new born.

END OF PART ONE

PART 2
2018
TO
THE PRESENT

1

The Present

Charlotte

Her glass and steel clothes shimmered. Her appearance was immaculate and her scent expensive. She was highly sought. Her manner was sophisticated. Summer escapades with her seemed like a distant dream. Then it began to rain. Her make-up started to wash away. I saw a glimpse of my old London then. I was happy that my childhood friend was still there and was only temporarily hiding under the glitz and glamour.

The rain had created mayhem. So no one took any notice of us. Above, thick, grey clouds and streams of golden and silver light followed us like spotlights from heaven. Sound flailed his hands in the wind. An unsuspecting beggar noticed the leaves and castaway plastic bags that followed Sound like whirling dervishes. Mr. C was overjoyed, like a boy in a theme park. He had travelled on every London route, underground and over ground, and had familiarised himself with every latest incarnation of the railway train.

Chandran and I peered through windows of cafés. They were a mosaic of relationships in this advanced world. Couples that canoodled, couples that fought, couples that didn't speak and many lonely people who were fixated on machines. The humble cup of coffee coped commendably from being an unprejudiced companion to ignored sidekick.

From one café to another, Chandran and I window shopped. I gaped at the unrestrained embraces and unrestricted kisses; Chandran eavesdropped on conversations. I love yous were uttered openly and gallantly. Encouraged, our fingers touched. Sound kept a record of the exact number. He relayed a commentary about it to our group like it were a tournament. We all laughed. It had been a long time since we had laughed together.

The lights above forked into ribbons of silver and gold. The clouds formed a guard of honour around them. The lights intersected over a large glass dome, which was a recent addition to the London skyline. It was where we were headed. The Carringham Gallery beckoned.

The roof that had stood there before had been retired. The installation of the artefact in the central atrium had brought about the necessary remodelling. The construction had involved twelve large military helicopters that ferried between them one hundred and eight discs. Each had descended into the central atrium of the building. The positioning had been precise. It had been supervised by a contingent of engineers on the ground and by skilled pilots in the air. Within hours, London had an indoor tower sheathed by a dome.

The tower, or Stele of Shu, was to be the highlight of an auction. It had caused the roof to be raised. The other star exhibit lined the walls of the central atrium and stretched longitudinally across five tall floors. They encircled the Stele in a cylinder of radiance. Referred to as the 'Walls of Gold', these were the tablets inscribed with the Tales of Shu.

I had been introduced to the tales through a humble bedtime story that Mama had told me. Today, inscribed in gold tablets, I was in awe of it. I worshipped it. Written in the enigmatic language of the Meluhhans, Shu's account of the people of Meluhha had been etched on a grand scale. As for the Stele, I had seen its fragments in several sacks and now, as it towered over us, I felt overwhelmed and overcome with a sense of fulfilment.

I felt tears run down my eyes.

'Laughter don't be emotional!' Sound announced loudly for the benefit of our group.

'Over here, Laughter, Moon and Mr. C,' Sound shouted. It transported me immediately to our classes in the plate room in Calicut. The names had been Mr. C's invention. I watched as Mr. C considered whether he should swear. He didn't. He just laughed. This moment was too precious. Our alumni were here together. My eyes followed Sound amidst the throngs of scholars, philologists, historians and security personnel. He stood behind a bench occupied by the three of the new incumbents: An archaeologist, a journalist and an Irish analyst. We had got to know them; us the mentors, them the mentees. They were a fine batch: the three of them and the auctioneer who now spoke.

'We open the bid for the first item, a girl's Victorian scrapbook, at a thousand pounds,' he announced.

The auctioneer looked at the audience; no one returned his gaze. Everyone stared down at the catalogue; some ignored it. But a handful felt sorry for my scrapbook and momentarily looked at it out of sympathy. There was an uncomfortable silence. A phone rang in the distance.

Six hundred seated heads turned. A woman rushed to a bank of desks in the corner of the room. Here, people sat, bent *over their registers, each with a phone in front of them. The audience hadn't noticed them until then. The woman had a piece of paper in her hand. They checked their lists. There was a surge of whispering. A consensus had been reached. The woman went to the auctioneer and pressed the note into his hand.*

'Sold,' he said softly, 'for thirty million, sixty-one thousand, eight hundred and fifty-seven pounds.'

The audience gasped in chorus. Chandran looked at me smiled. Sound guffawed. Gaugin and Van Gogh had been beaten by my book of doodles.

'The second item on the auction catalogue is a pocket tool circa early19ᵗʰ century.' The auctioneer looked at the audience for a starting bid. This time, they paid attention to the unassuming object held aloft by the auctioneer's nervous assistant.

Several copper labels held together by a single bronze clasp on one end and at the other, specially crafted appendages in metal to serve a number of purposes: needles, a fork, a spoon, a pick, a chisel and a knife. It had been Aaji's pride and joy.

'Do we have an opening bid on Item 2—a pocket tool from the mid-nineteenth century?'

This time, all the telephones rang at once. Sound exploded with laughter. Chandran mimicked a horrified look and Aaji had an impish expression. His pocket tool was causing a stir. The staff in attendance quickly scribbled on their registers, trying to keep pace with instructions supposedly barked at them from the other end of the phone line. The audience watched them with bated breath. The woman ran into the room again with her now famous piece of paper and submitted it to the auctioneer. He went to the desk of telephone operators and consulted with their registers.

This time, the auctioneer couldn't resist it. He lifted his head and smiled. On the paper was scribbled the bid amount, the same number: thirty million, sixty-one thousand, eight hundred and fifty-seven.

30 06 1857.

It was not just a number. It was the date when one chapter finished and another had begun.

2

New Beginnings

Sarah

It was a silent night. The sky wore a deep grey velvet skirt with a hem of white lace. It was where the water from the sea rose up in gentle frothing waves. There was a slight fog that levitated over the water. It created a sense of expectation. The moon rested on the sky's lap like a pearly white purse, hidden by a taffeta of clouds. A ship with an elegant figurehead drifted sedately into the port. The row of cedar trees on the brow of the hill waved to her in the light breeze. A star or two managed to peek out of sky's petticoats and saluted her. A blue butterfly was perched on the ship's crow's nest.

Her sails were draped over its many wooden masts. Within its hull, her cargo lay peaceful, enclosed within the fortifications of a hundred containers. The sleek ocean liners and container ships in the dock looked at her with envy. She was outdated yet dignified; her vintage wood and bronze contrasted with the sleek clinical lines of the new breed.

She was 'Mythili' and was specially commissioned to undertake a single to and fro voyage: A journey spanning twenty-two thousand nautical miles around the tip of Africa and through the currents of the Arabian sea and back. In her time, she was the largest that had ever been built.

Years later, her example was emulated with caution. Her proportions were envied but were never copied exactly. Not everyone was made for the life she would lead. While her contemporaries had busied themselves frequenting the exotic currents of the East, she waited patiently for her chance. When it came, she embarked with no fanfare. Her return on this day was even quieter.

The sun had begun its ascent. The gulls started their shrieking but even they observed a minute of silence, choosing to fly beside her rather than over her mast. The waves broke on her wooden hull with gentle caresses. She settled into a vacant spot in the port at Felixstowe and waited.

E dward Stanley Carringham was my great nephew five times removed. He was seated in a waiting room and was in no hurry. The doctor could take all the time he wanted.

The monitor strapped onto his heart had started beeping the previous night. Edward was mentally preparing a rather short guest list for his funeral when the doctor returned to his side, looking perplexed.

'It is strange. Your heart rate seems normal, strong even. There are five additional beats every minute on the ECG that

I can't explain.' the doctor said. 'It is best to continue with the monitoring and the medication. But otherwise, you are fine. No trips to Africa though.'

Albert, his trusted driver and personal assistant, rolled up onto the drive and watched intently as his master got into the car. Looking at Ed's glum face in the rear view mirror, Albert was relieved. His master had been waiting to die for years. But the man's grave countenance assured Albert that his boss, Edward Stanley Carringham, Earl of Saville, hadn't received that prognosis as yet.

The grand mansion had taken on the persona of its owner: disinterested and dreary. The majestic copper beech had seen three generations of the Carringhams. Its ancient branches were threatening to fall as it downsized to prepare for its final phase of retirement. The nettles had been given carte blanche and the unkempt garden played hostess to a party of daisies, dandelions, rabbits and crickets.

Cantankerous Edward was still affectionate, considerate and reminded me of my brother. The roaring business of the mid-nineteenth century had made us Carringhams one of the richest aristocratic families in the country. Out vast fortune—garnered from the spice trade—had been invested in London real estate, including a premier art gallery. But Edward lived a frugal life. His only significant expenses were his travels to the conflict- ridden corners of the world.

The family's shipping business had been retained but its management was entrusted to a private firm. Albert would sometimes ferry documents from the firm's offices for his master's signature. But this was the only part Ed agreed to play in the shipping business.

When they entered the house, Albert asked, 'Where will you be travelling to sir?' He got no reply from the despondent man. Instead, Ed walked to his desk wearily. Waiting for him on his desk was a summons from HMRC Customs. It made him furious.

His first stop was at the offices of the company that managed his shipping business. He made his way straight into the CEO's office.

'What am I paying you for, Mr. Merryweather? To warm that expensive Italian chair and to stare at the vulgar television screen?'

The CEO blinked at him. Edward waved the summons in front of him.

'Twiddling your thumbs and mooching around is exhausting isn't it? Surely I shouldn't expect you to keep tabs on my shipment and to respond to HMRC summons?'

With that delivery, Edward stomped off the premises and instructed Albert to drive him to the port at Felixstowe. He hadn't been there in decades. The yard of containers remained unchanged. They were probably just bigger and had a lot more international names. But in essence, it was still a haphazard collection of cuboids in different stages of wear. The ships stood in height order—the Chinese taller and heftier than its US and German counterparts.

Ships had come a long way from the East Indiamen I knew.

Edward barked at the smug customs official and showed him the summons. The customs official came back with the papers relating to the cargo and the ship. This time, it was the officer's countenance that was stirred. The date on the docket had the ship's departure date recorded as 30 June 1857. He flipped the pages this way and that. Every date on every page was signed with that same date. It seemed that the ship had set sail from Kozhikode on 30 June 1857 and arrived in England one hundred and sixty-one years later.

Edward signed the papers in disbelief. He asked for the customs manifest. The official's face clouded. The manifest of said ship had no names listed. The ship, it seemed, had made the journey all on its own with no crew.

'There must be a mistake,' said the man, mortified. Edward felt a lightness. It was an unfamiliar tugging at the edge of his lips. He felt a smile force its way up to his ears.

*T*he team Edward employed worked relentlessly. The cargo *in the first container was laid out on the extensive grounds of Edward's house. Two slits, the white of two eyes, peered out of a sea of black. Their gaze was not frantic but grateful—a hello from a civilisation so long ago that it almost seemed out of this world.*

All those years ago, when the tar had been used to coat the stretches of gold panels, the eyes of the Seer of Meluhha had defied the coating. Miles of turquoise and ivory marquetry, tourmaline embellishments and obsidian outlines still remained unexposed and hidden under the black lining.

For Edward, the Earl of Saville, the sight of those defiant pupils released happy memories of a childhood story. It was like a light had been turned on in an attic of fantastic people of an even more fantastic land.

Their blackness wasn't without reason. Layers of soot had been applied for their protection. It was also symbolic. For centuries, the truth had stood silently in the dark shadows. Generations of people had grown up around it, ignorant of benevolent giants of their past. But the time for a formal introduction was drawing to a close.

It would take a few weeks before all ninety-nine containers were emptied. He would have a glass pavilion erected over it and recruit an army of security guards to watch over it. Surveying the vast treasure, Edward felt like he had been given a second chance.

'Albert, ask your question again.'

'Where will you be travelling, sir?'

'Albert, I am going to India.'

Twenty-four years ago he had reached Kozhikode a week too late. The baby had been adopted by another family and he lost his chance of playing a part in her life. In a fit of rage and defeat, he had collated the evidence three generations of his family had pieced together and submitted his article 'Poseidon Heists' to the *Tribune's* office in India. It was a lapse of judgement, which he deeply regretted. It would not have taken long for the enemy to cover their tracks and morph into another company and infiltrate another country. The guilt had troubled him ever since.

But Edward was now a renewed man. His period of self-loathing and deriding was over. He would make amends. His doctor had told him that he had five extra unexplained heartbeats. He would go to India.

What Edward Stanley Carringham didn't know was that within a year, he would be dead.

Charlotte

I had travelled with her on that expedition a year ago. My ward had been a bundle of nerves and excitement. (My ward! It felt strange calling her that.) She was kneeling in a trench, re-examining the implement and trying to rid it of its stubbornly lodged gravel and grime. Their dig had been called off for the day. She should have been at base camp but she had disobeyed the curfew.

Earlier that day, Kalyani had discovered the storage pits at the bottom of a trench. Its structure had been beautifully preserved. She knew of storage pits that, in previous expeditions, had yielded treasures. She was disappointed to find it empty. The implement she found outside the pit filled her with anger.

Robbers, she thought. So many archaeological sites had been vandalised by greedy bandits looking to sell treasures in the black market. On closer examination, she was certain that the pocket tool was over a hundred years old. But this site had only been discovered recently so her bandit theory seemed implausible.

The question troubled her and suspicion gnawed at her all day. It was why she disobeyed curfew and came back to the site. Her re-examination of the trenches had produced further deviations. Fragments of pottery found in the same layer seemed different in style and composition. It went against the rules of stratification. She had been taught how objects, and sometimes structures, were found in layers of soil, along with other materials that had resulted from human activities. This sequence gave indications of the relative age of the styles of architecture and crafts. But she was certain the layers in the trenches she examined had been disturbed. If thieves had done it, they wouldn't have gone through the trouble of restoring the site after removing whatever they had been after. The more she thought about it, the more she was convinced that over a hundred years ago, someone had attempted to excavate this site. But why?

I recognised the place from Chandran and Aaji's description of Sindh. Surveying the terrain, I wondered how those two had survived the cruel elements of this godforsaken land. I sat a few yards away while Kalyani persevered with that pocket tool. She examined it. The sight of it made me laugh. Kalyani had found the tool Aaji had misplaced all those years ago. It connected her to our world. She was in the same place as my friends had been. Then a slow drumming began and I felt myself stiffen with fear.

It was Kalyani's first experience with the Team. Their team—a crew of American, Pakistani and Indian archaeologists—had been warned of the dangers. The rules were absolute. It was hostile territory and the curfew had been imposed for a reason. Dusk was approaching and she was growing increasingly desperate. She surveyed the surroundings, which were fast becoming opaque in the darkness. She surveyed the section of trenches that she hadn't checked yet.

I noticed a flicker in the distance. A lone turbaned and bearded man approached his bunker on the rocks. The turbaned man had spotted Kalyani's torchlight. The drumming reached a crescendo. The din of the percussion within me became unbearable. My anxiety produced a strong gust of wind that swept the sand into the trench and into Kalyani's eyes. I felt a tingling as I touched the torch. Kalyani was plunged into darkness. The darkness now cloaked her, protecting her from the Kalashnikov- wielding militant who had been assigned the task of taking out as many of the archaeology contingent as he could.

A year had passed since that incident. She had been suspended from site work because she had broken the rules. She had not shown the pocket tool to anyone for fear of being blamed for theft. It would have been the last straw.

As a teenager, Kalyani had been infatuated by the mystery of the Indus Valley. As an archaeologist, the enigma only deepened. Unravelling her wasn't going to be easy. The excavated sites grew in number—Kotla Nihang, Rangpur, Bahawalpur, Periano Ghundai, Dabarkot, Kulli, Nal and Amri—and so did the puzzles: the lack of a cemetery in Mohenjo Daro, the purpose of the great hall in Harappa, the absence of palaces, the lack of armaments and, the greatest mystery of all, a script that could not be deciphered.

She was under the spell of the Indus Valley script. Its toothpick forms occupied her every thought. She scanned the Sumerian, Etruscan, Hittite and Brahmi scripts for links, sometimes repeatedly going over the work of archaeologists before. It had only led to more questions.

There was a widely held theory that masses of historical evidence had been wiped out by the East India Company's quest to unify the country; and that they were destroyed by railway contractors during their quest for bricks. She, on the other hand, was driven by a gut instinct that the civilisation's treasure was out there somewhere, waiting to be unearthed. The discovery of that tool had strengthened that belief.

But ever since her suspension, her confidence had hit rock bottom. She doubted herself and had to look at the pocket contraption to remind herself that she hadn't imagined its presence in the trench. Was it possible that someone had removed the articles before the construction of the railway line? And if so, was it possible that a great proportion of the relics had been kept somewhere safe?

Kalyani heard a clap on her window. She first thought it was kids playing football, using her second-floor balcony window for goal practice. She ignored it. Then she heard another bang. This time, she was certain. She heard the sound of the handles of the widow being turned. Someone was trying to break in. She grabbed her badminton racket, using it as defence and wishing she had chosen baseball as a hobby sport instead.

Armed with her flimsy deterrent, she came eye-to-eye with the intruder—a monkey. He was large, hairy and white. Kalyani then noticed him gingerly remove his hand from a box of laddoos. *You petty thief,* she thought. He glanced at the racket and then at her. He got off the kitchen counter and lumbered towards her.

'Oh shit, shit, shit,' she mumbled under her breath. Her hands clutched the racket. She willed for it to start buzzing or fizzing or spraying. He was unphased. From under his arm came a fragile hand, followed by the small black face of a baby. Kalyani wasn't prepared for this. The pent up fear dissolved in an instant. The baby stretched its arms and put its palm on hers. A gentle high five!

The adult was a she—a mummy monkey. The two turned and headed towards the balcony. The mummy monkey reached for the latch of the window and pulled herself up. She looked back at Kalyani once. Kalyani smiled, her heart melting. In one quick movement, the mother reached for the laddoo box and helped herself to a single laddoo. The two disappeared.

Kalyani couldn't believe what had just happened. She returned the badminton racket to the cupboard. While doing so, she noticed a piece of paper stuck to her fingers.

Chandran

The doors opened. I leaned forward and peered into a small dining room. A boy sat at a table, looking out into a rose garden. His grandparents sat on either side. 'Kannan, eat something,' his grandfather pleaded. The boy didn't eat. His mind was fixated on the rose garden; it filled him with loss and dread.

The doors had opened on that same floor many times. Every time it was the same three people and they spoke very little. Even though time had passed, their pain was still present and palpable on every occasion: when the grandparents watched the boy sit by himself in a playground, when he refused to talk to anybody else and when he screamed and cried uncontrollably when the labourers came to pave the rose garden in his parents' house.

Ting. The doors opened. This time, I took two steps forward. The breeze felt good on my face. I was in a new environment—a newspaper office. Papers flew around. I lifted my hands. A red file fell into a box labelled 'Archives.' On that single occasion, there were no grandparents and no boy.

The visits into civilisation followed with greater frequency. The boy appeared in all my subsequent stops with unfailing regularity. His changing physicality made me aware of the passage of time. It made one other thing clear: He and I were bound to each other.

The doors opened again. It had been ten years. The boy and his grandparents were at his school. He had failed his tenth standard exams. His grandparents took him for ice cream at the 'India Coffee House'. They then went for his routine appointment to his psychiatrist and counsellor, as they had been doing for ten years.

After another shaft of silence, the doors opened again. This time, it was to my final stop. Lifts were awe inspiring. These mass transportation systems had given rise to incredible skyscrapers and transformed buildings into bustling galaxies. But I was glad when my elevator-like existence was over. I was finally home. My new home.

The boy was a man now.

Karthikeyan strolled into the Bangalore office of the *Tribune*. He didn't subscribe to the trend of 24/7 news reporting. He thought it was vulgar. At the age of 27, he had old fashioned values. He believed in honest journalism. His mobile was only for phone calls—social media was taboo. That morning, he walked in with a cup of hot chocolate, not the insipid black coffee and black tea that everyone else seemed to be incessantly sipping.

The flat screens and computers in the office flashed with images of the prime ministerial candidate, Deepika Pradeep. Mohan K's death had put his niece—the young, dynamic Deepika—at the helm of the party he had started 25 years ago—the Ram Rajya Party. Sceptics attributed her popularity and success to the sympathy factor that followed her uncle's tragic death.

His secretary handed him the courier that had been waiting for him for a week. Karthikeyan's breaks were famous. Some believed it was a spiritual retreat and his rivals believed he used the time to infiltrate. Either could be true because Karthikeyan always came back recharged and with a breaking story.

It had been the simple story of a children's daycare centre, run by a visionary, that catapulted him to fame. It was an ordinary establishment with an extraordinary recruitment policy—only grandparents could apply for jobs. He had an instinct about the story. It had struck a chord with him because of his own upbringing.

The story of the creche and its unlikely workforce attracted an unprecedented response from the newspapers' readers. It began the era of Page 1 heroes and heroines—common people with uncommon courage and strength of character. Overnight, Karthikeyan became Kannan, the darling of the masses and he who recognised beacons of moral strength.

Kannan had an innate ability to sense the story that lurked in one's eyes. He vetted his sources with the same penetrating ability as someone I once knew. It should have been little wonder then that Kannan was a descendant of the man I admired and respected—Kutty Ettan.

Kannan lifted the packet from the neat pile of papers. It was light. 'No tapes,' he muttered and sighed in relief.

He did not have the appetite to peruse video footage from vigilante groups today. The packet contained brownish pages torn from a registry of births and deaths. Five names were circled on the pages. A photo of Deepika Pradeep—the prime ministerial candidate from the Ram Rajya party—dropped out of the package.

Ranganath 'Chanakyan'. Birth: 3 March
1810; death: 30 June 1857

Raghavan Pattar. Birth: 15 June 1857;
death: 21 May 1930

Sukumar Pattar. Birth: 12 September 1898;
death: 14 July 1949

Giriraj Pattar. Birth: 11 December 1930;
death: 15 December 1990

Mohan K. Birth: 07 August 1954;
death: 14 February 2019

It was a family tree. Mohan K and his niece, Deepika, were
the harbingers of a new political dynasty. The name at the top
intrigued him. Ranganath 'Chanakyan'. He was sure he had
seen it somewhere. Kannan sat on his comfy seat and started
chewing on a pencil.

The harmless sheet of paper became an object of hate. A
single name evoked an intense and searing pain. Chanakyan
had the blood of two of my friends—Aaji and Chacko—on
his hands. The name on the paper gripped me with terror. The
pressure overwhelmed me and the terrorising name swam in
pools of blood before me.

A pool of scarlet liquid formed on Kannan's table and he
stared at it incredulously. He moved the paper and the puddle
followed. It slid over the paper and then stopped. He could
see the name Chanakyan through it. Kannan felt parched; an
uneasiness washed over him.

He wiped at it frantically, using a paper napkin. There was
no scarlet stain on the paper. Had he imagined it? He didn't
like the feeling. He folded the extract from the registry away

into his drawer and concentrated on an audit he had been postponing for days. The highly detailed spreadsheet had a mind-numbing quality, which he preferred on this occasion. But he couldn't ignore the constriction he felt in his head and chest. Soon, a phone call from Srinivasan put his mind in further turmoil.

A year ago, Kannan had interviewed Srinivasan, the proud owner of the telegraph machine. It was a relic from the Calicut Telegraph office and had become a recent addition to Srinivasan's collection of East India Company memorabilia.

'That telegraph machine has come to life!' Srinivasan said.

That morning, the long, decommissioned machine had, without warning, produced a single message. There were two words in the message, 'Chanakyan' and 'Poseidon' that had made Kannan almost fall off his chair. Kannan hesitantly typed the word 'Chanakyan' into the search engine bar and surveyed the results sceptically. For the second time that day, he was faced with the name. He repeated the process, this time searching for 'Poseidon & Chanakyan'

Dissatisfied, he used the *Tribune* database to do a quick search on 'Poseidon'. It returned a single entry: 'The Poseidon Heists', an article submitted by E. Carringham 25 years ago. He tried to access it but was unable to. A quick conversation with the editor revealed that articles that had been submitted and that weren't published weren't scanned into their database. The physical copies were returned to the author, stored in the archive or destroyed. There was something about this that gripped him with burning curiosity.

Kannan travelled to the old offices of the *Tribune*, surprised at his rashness. It was an ugly old building that had been forsaken for the new and polished premises on M.G Road. It still, however, housed the archives; they occupied an entire floor.

The floor was divided into four zones, each occupied by gigantic steel structures that carried folders covered in dust and cobwebs. The tube light over zone C flickered. It continued to flicker while Kannan walked across the floor, trying to determine where to begin. It had taken him almost half a day to comb through zone A and B. He was beginning to lose hope.

As he walked between the towering steel shelves, the flickering of the tube light stopped. Kannan stopped and looked up at it. From the corner of his eye, he saw a shelf whose sole occupant was a lonely red folder. Without a moment's hesitation, he grabbed the file and flipped the pages. The article by Edward Carringham, 'Poseidon Heists', seemed ordinary and unexceptional, lying in a fortress of steel.

Colin

Liam had been summoned to the plush office on the 27th floor of Number One Salisbury Park. He didn't even know the 27th floor existed. The elevators accessed by Triton's mere mortals only went up to the 26th floor.

To actually come face-to-face with the partner of his firm was like sighting a rare comet. The comparison wasn't farfetched. The man was an urban legend. In the financial crash of 2008, companies had crumbled. But not Triton. It had risen from the dust and was rescued from the jaws of administration under his stewardship. Liam was going to meet this genius.

The room was splendid. It reeked of expensive taste and an unlimited budget. The thirty-two seats around the conference table would have looked forlorn in the cavernous room had it not been for the beige Italian leather sofa suite, four flat screens and a contemporary crystal chandelier that stretched across the ceiling. Liam's eyes were focused on the three paintings behind his partner's head.

'Believe it or not, there is a woman hidden in these paintings,' the comet spoke first.

Liam stared at the paintings, not sure if this were a joke. 'So you contacted the inspector?' The comet didn't waste time. He was casually dressed in a linen shirt and chinos. His limited edition Breitling watch distracted Liam.

'Yes.'

'Actually, can we start from the beginning, Liam?'

'Edward Carringham went missing one year ago. Two weeks ago, his name appeared on the Bona Vacantia list and our radar. His last known whereabouts was a hotel in Kozhikode, where he checked in a year ago. According to the police report, Edward Carringham had booked a taxi to take him to a local church.'

'A church?'

'Yes. They said Edward was a religious man completing his formalities before checking out of the world.'

'Checking out of the world?'

'Those were the police inspector's words.'

'Did they think it was suicide?'

'Possibly. Edward knew his time was up. He was unwell. The medication in his baggage in his hotel room indicated a serious heart ailment.'

'The police are sure?'

'The inspector said it was an open and shut case.'

'So you think the answer is in the church?'

'Yes. If Edward knew he was dying, his last trip is significant. It could even lead us to his heir.' Liam stared into the eyes of the deer in the painting, looking for the mysterious woman.

'Wait here,' the partner said and left Liam unsupervised with the priceless art on the walls. He had told Liam that the paintings were a rare commission and a gift.

Liam sat, sizing up the room. It was plush and expansive. The floor to ceiling glass on two sides brought the London skyline to view. The dome of St. Paul's Cathedral still held its own. It would probably outlive its modern colleagues, which were all silhouetted to form London's iconic skyline.

In front of him, was the East Wing of Salisbury Park. It was separated from where he was by a ravine of steel and glass. He could see the spacious interiors of a room much grander than the one he was in. He saw the partner of his firm walk into that room. He spoke to a bald, fat man who was seated with his back to Liam. The folds of skin on the latter's neck bulged out of the collar of his shirt. On the wall in front of the bald man was an eye-catching floor to ceiling portrait of a person.

He watched with curiosity as the partner of his firm stood with his arms on either side, clutching at his pockets as though he were intimidated by the stout older man seated across him.

Their conversation was short and the seated man had done most of the talking.

Minutes later, the partner walked back into the room. 'You may proceed to Kozhikode. Keep me updated and good work.'

Liam wasn't paying attention. The events in the east wing room across had distracted him. The large portrait in the room opposite had fallen. The portly man bounced up and turned. Liam saw a face he didn't recognise.

But I did. My Liam was walking into the lair of the enemy.

*T*he events of that fateful day had played in an endless loop: we had watched Jim Burtenshaw die and then had proceeded to the Tharavdu and had emptied the contents of twenty bags of gun powder around the perimeter of our beloved home.

Chanakyan, Matheson and fifty or so arsonists and rioters plunged into our sanctuary. Through the window, we watched helplessly as Charlotte and Narayan Kutty walked into the crosshair of Matheson's rifle and fell to the ground, their bodies riddled with bullets. Lady Sarah stumbled to the floor at the sight, her hand lighting the fuse. Then everything fell silent. It was those memories that I needed to drown. The reason I haunted a run-down pub in Cork every evening. Until one day, the routine stopped. It was the day I saw Liam with Carly's unmistakable ginger curls and the letter in his hand.

*L*iam had come to Cork for the letter. Two years ago, he said goodbye to the place and boarded a train to London because his grandmother, Pammy, had died and there was nothing or no one to keep him in Cork anymore. Liam went to Catholic school for his education but Pammy had taught him life's lessons. On market days, she woke at 3:00 a.m. and baked batches of loaves.

Liam's lingering memory of his Pammy was of her pottering in the kitchen, stirring jam in one pot and treacly chutney in the other. A withered Victorian recipe book sat on top of a shelf. It was what had given rise to her business. The recipe for ginger '*puliyingi*' was one amongst several south Indian recipes that were popular at the industrial estate, where Pammy took the sandwich van, every lunch break.

On a Sunday, they would go to the Church of Sophia. Pammy would wear her stockings and Liam would see how the calloused skin of her feet and hands made holes in them. Yet those calloused hands had smoothed many a childhood calamity. Liam missed his Pammy, a name he had coined when he was an infant, combining Pam and Granny. The name had stayed. His Pammy fed almost every soul in Cork. Every street, every house and every park was a reminder of her. Together, they had walked the streets, hand-in-hand. So when she died he had to leave Ireland so he could heal from his loss.

But he had come back to Cork for the letter.

At the Sunday church sermons, he and Pammy had heard the story of Danny MacFayden—a folk hero and legend.

Danny had travelled to India and crossed paths with the Calicut Maharaja in the 19th century. It was the Maharaja's letter to the church that had told the story of his heroism and his fight against the East India Company.

It was the letter that had inspired a cherished dream for Pammy and Liam—to go to South India one day. Pammy would travel to the place that had inspired the author of her favourite cookbook while Liam would retrace the steps of Danny MacFayden.

Liam sought to obtain the letter from the church in Pammy's memory because it was a symbol of the dream they had together. So Liam had requested the Father of the Church of Sophia for a copy. The Father had obliged.

Was it the letter that had entranced me when I saw Liam at the pub that day? Had the Zamorin weaved magic into its words so that it would free me from the hole I had condemned myself to?

In that letter, Liam held a piece of me. The Zamorin had made me a hero. He didn't talk about how Danny MacFayden had abandoned his Irish identity for an English one or how I had been a dogsbody for the British East India Company and then a puppet for the Firm. My redemption had come on the day—30th June 1857—when I stood shoulder-to-shoulder with Chandran and her Ladyship and did what I knew was right.

As Liam took his instructions from the partner in that 27th-floor office, I had looked across the wing of the building, into the plush interiors of the conference room. I recoiled with horror as I recognised the person in the elaborate oil portrait.

And then I saw the face of the seated man as he turned towards us. One did not need a Masters in Genealogy or Genetics to know that the vile Burtenshaw species was intact and that the Firm was alive and even more dangerous in the hands of Lucas Burtenshaw, the latest successor.

3

Ghosts of Our Past

Sarah

I had to silence Jim Burtenshaw. It was why I forced the poison down his gullet.

The Burtenshaw family had wrecked our lives. While Jim Burtenshaw had ravaged my life, his uncle had played havoc in my grandfather's, who unwittingly financed his opium trade. When he disappeared with my grandfather's money the loss of the estate and the Earldom took a toll on my grandfather, driving him to bankruptcy and senility. My father had rebuilt the name and the fortune through trade with the Zamorin. Fate had brought us together again and again.

I had made a monumental decision that day. Not content with the murder of Jim Burtenshaw I decided to blow up the Maradu Tharavadu and all its innocent residents. It was the only way I knew to keep its secret safe and let everyone believe that whatever the Tharavadu protected had been destroyed. I had promised the Zamorin to keep Her safe.

But by virtue of that decision, I had the blood of the Tharavadu's residents on my hands. It was that action that determined my wretched fate in this world: I was cursed to be a silent bystander to the crimes of the latest Burtenshaw—Lucas.

Lucas Burtenshaw sat in the opulent conference suite that crowned the east wing tower. Situated on the 27th floor of Number One Salisbury Park, it had an uninterrupted view of the London skyline. The room was bisected by the two lead protagonists—the large portrait of Jim Burtenshaw on one end and Lucas, who sat at the head of the conference table in flesh and blood.

The latter was watching his latest business venture unfold on the expansive flat screen before him.

It was a busy market square in Cairo. Uniformed gunmen patrolled the region in jeeps. A bomb had gone off. The number of casualties and dead toll streamed across the screen. Earlier that morning, the final payment had been wired to the mercenaries who had delivered three months of anarchy in Cairo, as promised. Within a few weeks, Lucas Burtenshaw's friend would be installed as the premier of Egypt.

Lucas would unfold the plans for phase two to the board this morning. The contracts to rebuild Egypt would be awarded to every one of Poseidon's subsidiaries. It was a business formula that Lucas had applied to two other countries and perfected in Egypt.

Lucas looked at the portrait of his predecessor. Though they were separated by three generations, he felt a special closeness to Jim. The other photo he held dear was a group photo of business dignitaries. Amongst them was the bright-eyed face of his friend and business soulmate, Mohan K.

Thirty years ago, Mohan K visited England as part of the Indian Trade Commission. Lucas had been appointed as the Commission's chief contact. On their return from an industry excursion one late evening, Lucas's car crashed into a bicyclist, killing the latter instantly.

The car escaped unscratched with Lucas, Mohan K and a British MP intact. After a deliberation with the moralising British MP, it was decided that the MP would escort Lucas to the police station, where he would turn himself in. The next morning, in a freak accident, the elevator carrying the British MP crashed, killing him on the spot.

'A mere cyclist must not come in the way of your greatness,' Mohan had told him.

Mohan scored a lifetime's friendship with this first murder. It began their business partnership and friendship for years to come. It also became fortuitous in realising the Burtenshaw vendetta.

When he was a teenager, Lucas had learned that Jim Burtenshaw's death in the mid-nineteenth century had been no accident. He discovered that Jim Burtenshaw had moved his base of operations to India in the early 19th century. Jim had begun to divert funds from Egypt and Iraq. Jim's abrupt death, however, caused the business empire to collapse. His plan for India was known only to a couple of men he trusted, all who were killed on the same day—30 June 1857.

The only clues were the four names he had found in Jim Burtenshaw's Journal.

- James and Lady Sarah Carringham
- Vikraman Varma, the Zamorin
- Narayanan Kutty—Zamorin's right hand man

The four names formed the core of his vendetta. As the Zamorin's bloodline had been terminated with his death, Jim Burtenshaw's death would be avenged by the elimination of two families: the 21st-century descendants of Narayanan Kutty and Lady Sarah Carringham.

Mohan traced Narayanan Kutty's bloodline to a journalist couple who had created their own news portal. Mohan lured them into a story they couldn't resist and supervised the killing himself. It was Mohan's idea that the bodies be buried in front of the couple's six-year-old son, in their rose garden.

In the case of Lady Sarah's descendant, Lucas had taken it upon himself to finish him off. It seemed no help was required on this quarter as Edward Carringham was a man on the path of self-destruction. But then he planned a journey to India, which piqued Lucas' interest. Mohan promised to take care of it and Lucas agreed. But he had wanted to see for himself.

Lucas had followed Edward Stanley from the hotel in Kozhikode to the Infant Jesus Church exactly a year ago.

He watched as Edward spoke with the nun and then made his way, on foot, to the busy Kozhikode bypass. Lucas tried to call Mohan but no sooner had he rung his number than a minibus jostled past Edward and came to a halt. Three men clad in black jumped out and pushed Edward into a van. The events of the day of Edward Carringham's kidnap were blurry.

His secretary's entrance disturbed Lucas from his stupor. 'I am sorry, Mr. Burtenshaw,' the secretary said apologetically. 'It is about Edward Carringham.'

The Partner of Triton walked into the room. Lucas had acquired Triton during the recession. 'It's Edward Stanley. You asked me to let you know when we have confirmation. His name is on the Bona Vacantia list. If we take care of the heir, we should be able to pocket half a billion from his estate.'

'There is an heir?' Lucas was not expecting this.

'Edward Stanley visited a church in Kozhikode before he died.'

Lucas knew this already. 'And?' he asked impatiently.

'It was a church and an orphanage.'

Lucas felt his chest swell. He was transported to the hot, humid day in Kozhikode. He had witnessed Edward Stanley's kidnap and satisfaction had engulfed him. He remembered seeing the back of the nun's starched habit and her hand extending to Edward, taking the letter from him. It was an orphanage. He had overlooked that detail. There must have been a child. Why else would Edward Stanley visit it?

Was it possible that the Zamorin's bloodline had not finished with the death of the Zamorin?

'Send your employee to Kozhikode.' The partner left the room swiftly.

Lucas looked at Jim Burtenshaw's portrait. He felt a surge of triumph. The Carringhams and the Zamorin had a special connection 160 years ago—a relationship Jim Burtenshaw had been striving to uncover. Was it possible that their connection went beyond business?

The sudden loud crash made Lucas jump. He squealed in pain as his weight pressed on his knee. A sudden gust of wind had swept up from under the long table and knocked the portrait of Jim Burtenshaw off its hook. It came crashing down. Lucas looked around. The windows of the conference room were firmly shut. The wind had come from nowhere.

I unhooked it and allowed it to crash to the ground. Although I regretted not having crushed the portrait into smithereens, I savoured the fear I saw in Lucas's eyes. I was a bystander to his actions but no longer a silent one.

Charlotte

In a vortex of darkness, the voice was my only companion. The only one that knew I existed and the only one that I could rely on. The voice provided orientation, beginning with short trips. But it always returned me to my shell.

Shell. That is what I called it. It was my sanctuary from what surrounded me and unnerved me. Slowly, the journeys became longer, their duration steadily increasing. Each journey was through a new landscape, the images blurred but still coherent. It was like I was travelling through them at a gallop.

The first excursions had been to the expansive grounds of a mansion. A girl played in the lawns while her mother watched her affectionately. In a window near the top of the house, a handsome man busied himself with coloured liquids in a glass apparatus.

The surroundings changed dramatically on subsequent trips. There was a cornucopia of colours, sights, sounds and smells. There were beautiful and intricate buildings, the elaborate lunch and the old man with his sparkling earrings. There was the lantern-like house and the handsome Indian boy, the emerald green waters of the pond and a teacher and his umbrella. The same boy and a girl sat under an enormous tree with a name etched on its bark— my name.

The inner voice had taken me through memories that had been preserved in me and provided an anchor in the sea of the unknown. My orientation was complete. I discovered then that the shell, the space I considered my sanctuary, had been my scrapbook. How I had come to be entwined in my scrapbook, I did not know.

But my journey with my ward had begun on the steps of the Infant Jesus Church. From then to now, I had not left her side for a minute. When a grown-up and career-driven Kalyani had parted from her scrapbook, I remained by Kalyani's side. Why? Because I had been instructed to do so by my father. Written on the first page of the scrapbook, in my father's hand, were his words:

'Molu, for your protection.'

Kalyani found the scrapbook where she had left it all those years ago—in the house of her adoptive parents. It remained on her bookshelf, amongst other knick-knacks that she had outgrown. She had booked her tickets to Bangalore, boarded a train and arrived in her parent's home all done five minutes after a monkey's visit. Yes. Five minutes after receiving a missive from a monkey.

'Find your scrapbook,' the note had read. What did this mean?

How did the monkey know of the scrapbook?

A monkey?

Was she losing a handle on reality? Had the suspension from her job made her mad?

She flipped the pages of the scrapbook and turned it this way and that. There were pieces of faded silk, brightly coloured feathers, buttons and sketches of a girl and a boy. Repeated sketches of elephants gave way to more deliberate and focused drawings. She flicked through the pages faster. Pencil strokes merged with each other. She repeated her actions as though hypnotised. The jagged lines developed into more certain contours as if the illustrator were developing their skills through the pages of the book.

But it wasn't one illustrator. It was two. I recognised my crude drawings as well as my father's, embedded between the pages. When had he done this? And more importantly, why? My eyes glazed over as Kalyani turned the pages even faster.

Kalyani impatiently dropped the book on the table.

I grabbed the book before it hit the surface. The pages barely touched my fingers. They flashed this way and that. I skimmed through them, my fingers stretched over the cover while my thumb curled under the pages, letting one drop after another. First, slowly and then quickly.

A drawing of a small figure caught my eye. It was drawn at the bottom of the page. He sat behind bars in the first page. With each page, he moved closer and closer until the bars were behind him. I thought of my father in prison in Calcutta. That realisation was immediately overtaken by another one. Had he been freed? Or had he escaped?

Kalyani sat on her bed, hypnotised. Her eyes peeled, looking at the book that seemed to live, breathe, move and levitate over the table in front of her. It turned its papery appendages relentlessly to show her something she recognised. Then it stopped. She knelt on her bed and craned her neck. She wasn't afraid of the enchanted book. Her lack of fear astounded her. But she didn't dare go near it. Not yet. From where she sat, she could see a family portrait.

Papa had drawn our family—Acchachan, me, Mama and him—together in one picture. The source of my papa's dimples was infinitely clear in Acchachan's dimpled smile. Through this sketch of our family, had Papa wanted to tell me about my grandfather?

The pages of the book slumped. Kalyani approached the book and held it gingerly. She turned the pages and scanned them, this time patiently. She looked over the sketches of people, animals, temples and an elephant. It was the same elephant again and again. She looked at the drawings and then jerked her head up. What she saw outside the window left her speechless.

A pachyderm had sauntered over to the gate of the two-storeyed modest house in this Bangalore suburb. She squeezed her trunk through the bars of the gate and looked directly at Kalyani, who stood transfixed at her window.

Just like that day in 1852 when Janani had arrived unexpectedly at the Tharavadu to welcome us into the fold, she had arrived here too with a similar intention. She dipped her trunk into the pond and lifted her trunk in preparation to baptise Kalyani.

The pink and grey speckled trunk had walked out of the pages of the scrapbook and into Kalyani's garden. The pachyderm looked at Kalyani with smiling, twinkling eyes while Kalyani worked out if she were awake or asleep. Kalyani watched, mesmerised as the water droplets from the pachyderm's majestic trunk magnified around her, each suspended at different levels, orbiting around her in slow motion.

Through the sheer walls of one droplet, she saw the lantern shaped house and a five stemmed bronze lamp in the other. In one, she saw a single lamp lit in front of a hovel. In a multitude of other bubbles were reflections of hundreds of flickering lamps. Kalyani felt like she was surrounded by satellites. Drawings from the scrapbook lifted into the countless glass spheres around her.

Suddenly, the sound of the temple conch reverberated through the room. It sounded like the commencemnt of evening prayers in the Thali temple at dusk. Aaji and Chandran bolted past me. I recognised their temple dash. I almost touched the Tulsi and Rajnigandha as it spun across the air, from behind Aaji's ear. It was a five-minute sprint to the Thali temple where they rang the bell outside Shiva's shrine.

In a flash, they were back. They dashed through the gates of the gatehouse. I watched as the specks of ash and sandalwood fell from their foreheads and rested precariously on the tips of their noses as the two burst through the gatehouse. The shade of the rubber tree, the fragrance of the champakam and the cool evening sea breeze had drifted into our room.

The four walls of Kalyani's bedroom merged into the compound wall of my beloved Tharavadu. The small brown doors of the shrine opened. Aaji and Chandran had made it in time for the evening prayers to our Goddess—Goddess Sita, who resided in the Tharavadu temple. Damayanthi's arm relentlessly rang the bell. I saw the tattoo on her arm turn a flaming red as she continued to ring the bells in a trance. I had never seen that before.

The tattoo rose from the arm of a woman drawn on the scrapbook. It was a vine entwined around a dagger. Kalyani recognised it immediately. It was a symbol she had catalogued during an excursion; it had been found on the sarcophagus of the unidentified scholar that had been recovered in a

Sumerian tomb. He had not been identified as yet. There were many legends about the man.

'He who lived at the time of the great Meluhhan cataclysm.' 'He who knew several languages'

'He who was the greatest translator.'

It was rumoured that he had commissioned a translation table.

'It cannot be. It is not true.' Kalyani muttered. She closed her ears to shut out the noise of a thousand bells and a temple conch that had come from nowhere. She shut her eyes to ward off the tantalising outline of the symbol. She beseeched her mind to stop playing games with her. It had always been her cherished belief that a translation table existed—the Rosetta of the Indus Valley that would decipher the Indus Valley script.

But the setback of the suspension and the ordeal of losing her colleagues' trust had crushed her confidence and made her question her thoughts. She was scared that the pain, frustration, stinging disappointment and her anger had created fertile ground for her mind to embellish reality with fabrications. She collapsed onto her bed, her hands pressing against her eyes as she willed herself to not look at the scrapbook again.

The drumming continued, this time with greater intensity. The shade and breeze were now replaced by burning heat. I saw Papa behind bars. Then Papa drank a liquid from a vial and collapsed. Two sentries pushed his body into a river. He sank but only for a brief instant. He swam across that great grey river. Papa had come home. He hadn't died in Calcutta. He had escaped. He looked into the compound of our beloved Tharavadu.

Bullets bounced and bodies dropped. A young girl came into view and the man with her tried to form a human shield between her and the gunmen. I felt a searing pain as the girl collapsed. I didn't need to see her face to know it was me. I watched as Narayanan Kutty turned towards the gunman and struck him, his own body perforated by countless bullet holes.

The Tharavadu exploded in front of me with all the people I loved: Mama, Chandran, Mr. C, Radha, Krishnan Kutty, Subhadra, Girija. The flames grew hotter and faster. There were no shrieks, just the smouldering of wood, the hissing of flames and the whooshing of wind as it caressed the smoke. It was the last thing I heard and saw before darkness and oblivion descended. But Papa had been there and had witnessed it all.

Kalyani felt the floor under her feet vibrate. The scrapbook thrummed against the surface of the table, like a dragonfly flapping its wings against a window. It sputtered and grated like a spinning movie reel.

The scrapbook splayed open to reveal a sketch of the deity of the Tharavadu shrine. It was Goddess Sita. I had never seen her this close before. Papa had drawn her here, in the book. Then the pages turned again. The metal sheet that clad the stone statue dissolved into the ground and revealed a hole. The pages turned faster, sucking me into that black hole.

I found myself fall a great depth, broken suddenly by a blinding light. The light mellowed around a large brilliant golden core. As my eyes grew accustomed to the brightness, the outline became clearer. It was a colossal cylindrical tower. On its outer façade was the intricate carving of a woman seated on a lotus. One of her hands was raised with her palm open and upright, in a gesture of giving blessings. Her other hand was on a bow that rested on her thigh.

It was the Goddess a hundred times bigger and a thousand times more radiant. The statue we had worshipped in the shrine had just been a symbol. The true Goddess resided deep underground. She lay in the rocky subterranean surroundings, more brilliant and breathtaking than the form we had worshipped in the Tharavadu temple, hundreds of metres above. Next to the colossal tower, I saw Papa's lifeless form.

Kalyani's eyes were dazzled by the tower of fire that had emerged from the book and formed a column of radiance in the middle of her room. Kalyani's body grew stiff as she watched symbols she knew so well emerge from the golden cylinder. The sequence of Indus Valley characters circled it, dividing it into discs. They alternated with rings of cuneiform symbols.

Tears ran down her face as she pieced together what it meant—the presence of a known script and an unknown script. It was a translation table from the Sumerian form to Meluhhan. But the translation table was a legend. Could it be true? The din of temple bells and temple drums had vanished. The scrapbook lay lifeless. The silence was deafening. The spinning golden core had vanished.

She looked out of the window. The elephant had disappeared. But her hands were wet. She wiped them on her jeans. They were wet too. She was, in fact, soaking. The elephant had showered her with water from the pond. She had not imagined it.

Sarah

This was my resting place. It was dark and musty and reminded me of a station's waiting room. In many ways, it was. It was a retreat from my trips through the dark underbelly of society. A traveller had joined me. I recognised her despite her stark attire. Her graceful features and the bronze face were still enchantingly beautiful.

A small flicker of light came on. A dark underground expanse transformed into a vista of columns. It illuminated the archway that stood like a brickwork giant that joined hands with the outstretched arms of other columns. From the limited reach of the torch, it was impossible to tell that these giant archways continued like that for miles. But they did.

She knew the place well. She had known it for many years. She descended the steps slowly and stopped when she reached the fourteenth step. She held onto the wall, sat down and immersed her left foot in the water. The gentle waves lapped against her feet. Holding the wall with one hand, she reached out for the edge of the wooden raft. She carefully got into it and lifted the oars. The chamber's thousand pillars towered around her. She circled them on her raft, the light from her torch illuminating the symbols carved on them. The beam danced on the surface of the water and refracted on the smooth pillars. She shone her torch up to see the crown of the pillars, which were ornately carved. The mosaic tiles that made the intricate pattern on the ceiling glimmered from the snatches of light.

After meandering through the columns, she arrived at the edge of the chamber. The corridor ahead of her—one amongst a hundred—was narrow and lined with a frieze on both sides, depicting the elephants. The water was deeper here; the swimming carp produced bubbles that made their way to the surface and reminded her that she was not utterly alone.

She reached for the packet of bread and let its crumbs fall into the water. The splashing and shimmering of fins reminded her of the baby she had brought here when she was only a few days old. The fish had entranced the child. The fish now followed her raft like a throng of pilgrims.

She approached a large column. Carved onto it was the bearded man with a ribbon of gold on his head. He evoked a feeling of wellbeing and peace. He stood at the entrance to the innermost chamber which was the most sacred of all. The height of the chamber amazed her. Light penetrated from a slit in the ceiling, several floors above. These walls were not ordinary; their stone was arranged to form stairs that lined the entire chamber. This was a stepped well.—a rare example of the architecture employed by ancient people to reach underground sources of water. The water at the base was the brilliant blue of an opal. Small stone mounds rose from its surface, each flat face holding remnants of the previous day's offerings.

She reached into the boat for her bag and then stepped out of it, immersing her legs in the cold blue waters. She removed the withered *thethchi* from the mounds and replaced it with flowers she had plucked from the garden earlier that day. She twisted a clean white cotton wick and pressed it into the earthen lamp and refilled the oil. She lit the lamp and moved on, following the same procedure for all the mounds. She arrived at the furthest end of the well and exclaimed. The congregation of stone mounds before her were newer than the others, the granite still blue. Their surfaces were clean.

'A stone mound for every Guardian spirit,' she muttered the words.

The sunbeam that had bathed them in a muted golden glow struggled through a narrow vent, several hundred metres above. She thought of the prayers that had been said and the offerings that had been made in the shrine above. Her hands pulsated as though she were ringing the bell.

The far end of the chamber was sealed by a large bronze door. The elaborate gold lock spread across it was inscribed with the familiar pattern of the dagger and leaves. She placed a lamp at the foot of the door with a cotton wick drenched in oil. She lit it and muttered a prayer. The garland she had made with the *thetchi*, *thulasi* and jasmine she hung over the lock. The smoke of the flame entwined with the fragrance. It found its way through the keyhole in the door and ventured into territory that no one had set foot into after that fateful day—30 June 1857.

Behind those towering bronze doors was my husband's parting gift to the world.

The woman did not disturb them. The sacred chamber behind the doors was where a Guardian had spent his last hours assembling the Stele. His body had since dissolved. In its place, a granite mound had pierced through the ground. The fragrance of the garland and the warmth of the lamp she lit would wrap around the granite and waft into the cavernous space around it. It would also brush against the colossal installation of the Stele.

The Guardian had made it his life's mission to reassemble Shu's Stele. Hundreds of years ago the disciples of Shu had scattered its constituent parts for its protection. The map had helped in its retrieval. Still, the greater challenge had been to bring it all together. There was a trick behind its assemblage. The Guardian had worked this out during his imprisonment in Calcutta. It was his hunch that Shu-Ilishu, being a devout man, would offer his greatest work to the Earth Goddess.

The segments of the Stele had been designed so that they interlocked and created the form of the Goddess. Although he had mentally solved the puzzle, there was the daunting task of physically assembling the millions of pieces. His helpless situation filled him with agony. It was not just the physical pain inflicted from his imprisonment and the torture of seeing everyone he loved perish before his very eyes. He was faced with the utter hopelessness that he knew the secret to assembling the great puzzle of the Stele but was running out of time to humanly realise it.

In his last moments, he hoped desperately that the frantic sketches he had made in the scrapbook, of the Goddess with its rings of symbols in Cuneiform and Meluhhan, would find their way to deserving hands and they would find a way of completing it. He had intended it for his daughter. But the truth was that there was no human way to assemble the thousands of pieces. The segments only needed to be near one another. Such was the ingenuity of the construction that they assembled themselves automatically. A thousand mechanical hands, feet and wheels had emerged from the segments and had interlocked with each other. All they had needed was for their constituents parts to be close to each other.

It was fitting that the Guardian's cenotaph lay at the feet of the colossal Stele.

The woman turned to leave. A gentle breeze blew over the mounds. It teased the flames of the lamps that had been placed on each granite shrine and she knew she was not alone. She turned around and smiled.

*As she faced me, seated on the steps of the stone well, I noticed that she—***Damayanthi***—looked well.*

Damayanthi came out of the old Dutch factory. It still stood defiantly after all these years, hiding a secret in its belly, stretching for miles in a labyrinth of numerous corridors. Her eyes quickly acclimatised to the bright sunlight. She glanced at the ordinary chaos that unfolded around the Mananchira Tank. It was chaotic. There was the melee of stuffed buses, screeching motorbikes, reckless cyclists and cars that provided the soundscape of Kozhikode. She walked at a brisk pace along the *Maidan* and headed straight for the Infant Jesus Church.

Colin

No sooner had Liam touched down at the Calicut airport than he made his way to the food court. He scanned the menus at all the restaurants. When he found what he was looking for, he placed an order confidently. 'One plate of vada, please. Does it come with Ulli Samandhi?'

I was proud of my boy. For one, he pronounced vada a hundred times better than I ever did. The other, he had a heart of gold. Liam hated to experiment with food. The more predictable and bland, the better. But Pammy loved variety. The more experimental, spicier and tangier, the better. It had been their dream to visit Calicut together. (Calicut had since changed its name to discombobulating Kozhikode.) And so Liam was bent upon living it up for both of them and if that meant ordering Vada and Samandhi when he himself would have ordered toast, then so be it. And I had tagged along too to visit my second home.

At the Infant Jesus Church in Kozhikode (Calicut), a nun brimmed with enthusiasm and helpfulness. She had told Liam that Edward Carringham had been to the Infant Jesus Church first in 1994 and then again in 2018. In 2018, he had left a letter for Baby Pongal. She had not given Ed the child's address but had offered to post the letter for him.

'I named her,' she said proudly. 'Where I come from, *Pongal* is an auspicious day and is my favourite festival. That is why I called her that.'

The nun recounted the events of the day she found the baby on the steps of the church, swaddled in embroidered cotton with an unlikely companion—a scrapbook. The baby had been sheltered in their orphanage and had since found a loving home.

The nun had shown Liam an old register with enthusiasm. She pointed to an entry on the page. It was from 25 years ago, a month after Baby Pongal was found on the steps and barely a week after she had been adopted. There had been an enquiry for Baby Pongal and beside the name on the register was the neat signature of Edward Carringham.

Liam returned to the hotel, feeling satisfied. He left a voice mail for his case manager, summarising his findings. He was certain that his work was done. It was obvious that Mr. Carringham had an interest in Baby Pongal. Baby Pongal, obviously no longer a baby, would provide the clues and perhaps lead to the heir. He typed an email to his line manager. His bosses at Triton would be pleased with his progress.

Liam carefully attached the Bangalore address that he had discretely photographed from the orphanage's register when the nun wasn't looking. He was proud of his resourcefulness. He clicked on the send button a few times but his laptop was having one of its moments. *I will come back to it*, he thought and curled up on the sofa after placing an order with room service. A newspaper was slipped under his door just as he had made himself comfortable.

Liam was drawn to an article in the newspaper and the sepia photograph accompanying it. It contained a black and white picture of three East India officials surrounding a telegraph machine with their names listed below. The name in the centre made Liam jump. Colin Coquettish. It was a name he knew well. It was the alias acquired by Danny MacFayden.

Liam was staring at a photo of me. It wasn't the most flattering and my nose looked awfully big.

The date of the newspaper made Liam feel uneasy. It was from a year ago. It made his heart race and his skin tingle. He opened the door and looked outside. There was no one there. He was almost relieved. What was he expecting to see? He called the reception. They had no knowledge of where the newspaper had come from.

'Sir, can I send some snacks for your guest?'

'Guest?'

'She arrived an hour earlier. She knew your room number so we let her come up.'

Someone, a woman, wanted him to have the paper. He looked at the article and jotted the name of the journalist. 'Kannan.'

Chennai, Liam's latest destination, was a larger, shriller and hotter version of Kozhikode. There were loudspeakers mounted on almost every second auto rickshaw, van and truck, blaring the shrill political address of candidates. Election season in India was like the festival of Holi. Only, instead of a riot of colours, it was a riot of varying decibels. His overnight train journey had allowed him no sleep.

Liam clutched the paper bearing the address. The auto rickshaw driver had scant regard for life, evident by the way he took on the traffic that attacked him from all directions. Liam sat unsteadily on the auto seat, sliding from edge to edge, his brain being rattled like nuts in a mixer grinder.

Liam had called the directory enquiries and obtained Kannan's number. He didn't stop to think or consider his next action. He dialled the number, half expecting it to ring out.

'Hello.'

'Oh,' Liam said, caught by surprise. He hadn't been expecting anyone to answer and now he felt stupid. 'I had a question on the article about the telegraph machine. The one you wrote a year earlier.'

'The one that woke up?' asked the voice on the other end. 'Woke up?'

This wasn't a response he was expecting.

'Yes, it had been decommissioned, disconnected and sold at auction to a Colonial Engineering aficionado. It woke up this morning and spat out four random names.'

'I see.' Liam did not know what to make of this.

'Isn't that why you called?'

'No. I had no idea. You said this telegraph machine gave out names?'

There was a silence. Liam realised he wasn't going to get information from a journalist unless he spilt some first. 'I work with Triton, a probate firm in London. I was in Kozhikode, investigating the case of Edward Carringham when I happened on your article.'

'Edward Stanley Carringham?' The voice on the phone had become louder and excited.

'You know him?'

It was the conversation with the journalist that made Liam brave the journey from Kozhikode to Chennai that very night. Kannan had suggested they meet at the *Tribune's* Chennai office, where Liam now waited, feeling apprehensive. Kannan brought a paper cup of piping hot coffee and his own cup of hot chocolate. He pushed the coffee into Liam's hand and thrust the red folder titled '***Poseidon Heists***' into Liam's other hand.

Kannan sat across him and pointed to the folder. 'This is the article I told you about. It was submitted by Edward Stanley Carringham. It was the name 'Poseidon' and 'Chanakyan' in the telegraph's message that led me to it. Twenty-five years ago, Edward submitted the article. But it didn't make it to the editor for his review. It went missing. But I found it in our archives.'

'Have you read it?' Liam asked. 'It looks more like a case file than an article,' Liam observed from the thickness of the volume.

'I have flicked through it. I don't know what to make of it. The machinations of a very creative and eccentric brain or the very twisted and macabre dealings of an ancient enterprise.'

'Ancient how?' Liam asked.

'There is a chapter on the privateering and the dark slave trade. That would put its inception around the same time as the Royal Charter of 1600.'

'And slave trade wasn't their only dodgy dealing?'

'Edward writes of criminals that vanished into thin air in the mid-nineteenth century. He claims that they were all reintroduced into society with a brand new face and identity. To me, that reads plastic surgery. But plastic surgery in the 19th century?'

Liam was unable to answer.

'Then there are pages and pages of lists: lists of documents forged, antiquities and paintings stolen.'

'Perhaps we start with the lists?' Liam was unsettled by his calm response. Had the Chennai air messed with his head? Was he really going through with this?

'I tried. But I could not make head nor tail of it. These are lists of forged Egyptian and Mesopotamian manuscripts several thousand years old. We would need to hire a historian, specialist or whatever and travel to Alexandria, Iraq or even Syria.' Kannan shuddered at the thought, his mind calculating the expense and risk and visualising his director's disapproval.

'What about the paintings?' Liam asked.

'I don't recognise the paintings. They are possibly priceless artworks that were never catalogued in the first place— syphoned off private collections by thieves and fraudsters. I don't know. On the face of it, it seems like a wild goose chase, as if Edward is watching us and laughing at us gullible idiots. But a big part of me is goading me to believe it and find sense and logic in it.'

Liam felt the same. He was tempted to talk of Danny MacFayden, aka Colin Coquettish. The picture in the article that had made him call Kannan in the first place. Was this stupidity or fate?

Liam picked up the red file and started flicking through it. The list of forged documents had been neatly indexed and labelled. Either Edward had spent years collating this information or his brain had concocted a very convincing table. He was taken aback by the meticulous catalogue of paintings that followed—thousands of titles arranged by place and date. He recognised some of the places: the princely provinces of Travancore, Mysore, Kashmir, Hyderabad and Calicut. He turned to the page with the paintings of Calicut. The Bow—EC; the Deer—EC; the Fire Sacrifice—EC.

'I have seen three of these paintings,' Liam blurted. Kannan stared at him. 'What?'

'I have seen the three paintings in my partner's office in London.'

'The same ones?'

'I saw the three with the same titles and artist, all together in one place. I remember them well. In one, the face of a woman is in the eyes of a deer, her silhouette in the lustre of the bow and the flames of a sacrificial pyre. The partner said it had been a gift.'

Liam remembered the day distinctly. It was the first time he had met the partner. It was the day he had been instructed to travel to Kozhikode.

'Gifted it?' Kannan was pacing up and down the plush reception. In all the excitement, Kannan had forgotten to escort Liam to his office upstairs. Passers-by watched, making Liam feel slightly conscious.

'Yes, gifted after an acquisition, a 'welcome to the club' present.' Those were the words the partner had used. Liam paused. He was thirsty. The air conditioning irritated his throat.

'Tell me about your company,' Kannan said.

'In the crash of 2008, many companies folded. But not Triton. It came out stronger. The managing partner is still revered as a legend—the man instrumental for turning it around. It is said that he engineered the acquisition which saved it.'

'What was the name of the acquiring company?' Kannan asked.

'I don't know,' Liam replied. 'The partner comes from a very well-connected family. Perhaps they were involved.'

Kannan stopped pacing. He looked at Liam with a smile on his face. 'In Greek mythology, Triton is the son of Poseidon.'

Liam looked at Kannan. He laughed when he made the connection. 'The Poseidon of Poseidon Heists?' he asked, pointing at the folder. But Kannan was serious. As he replayed the sentence in his mind, his face became more taut and he began to believe it more and more.

'Wait a minute. Are you saying what I think you are saying?'

'Yes, I mean we can always check with Company House. I can bet you that the name registered for the parent company, the acquiring company will be something else, an alias. But I can't seem to shake this hunch. It seems we are all connected—Poseidon, Triton, Edward, you, me, Chanakyan, Mohan K and the next prime minister of India.'

Liam looked at him. He remembered the conversation they had on the phone. How the names on the pages torn from a death registry had connected a 19th century hit man—Chanakyan—and the person who was tipped to win the Indian elections per the exit polls.

'So what do we do?'

They both looked at each other. The bustle of the lobby and the road outside blurred in the background. Everything else faded. It was just the two of them and the red folder.

Kannan spoke. 'We need to be sure.'

Liam took out his phone and thumbed through his photos quickly. The address he had photographed from the nun's register was still there. 'Baby Pongal. She holds the key. I have her address. Edward had written her a letter.'

'So she could be an important piece of the jigsaw. Either that or this whole thing is an elaborate con?' Kannan looked at the address on the phone and made a quick calculation.

They became aware of their surroundings. It was only when they looked outside that they noticed darkness had descended.

'So are you putting me up in the lobby for the night?' Liam asked.

'Unfortunately for you, it will be another night on a train, my friend.'

The word 'friend' warmed him. In Chennai, with temperatures of 36 degrees, that was no miracle. But it was a déjà vu that struck him. It was of a situation so familiar but so hard to recollect.

Kannan was walking and talking. They had left the building and were making their way to an auto stand. Liam went over the events of the last week. Three weeks ago, he was barely tolerating the mundane tube travel of London. Three weeks hence, he was savouring the myriad modes of transport in a country on the other side of the globe. There was no rational explanation, just events that had been written and destined to occur.

It was Kannan who spoke. 'The words on the telegraph, 'Chanakyan' and 'Poseidon', led me to the article and, in a manner of speaking, to you as well. But there were these other two words which make me wonder if that was someone's idea of a joke.'

'What were they?' Liam asked. He sensed his breath quickening,

'Tamarind Tiger! I mean, who would put that in a telegraph message?'

Liam's jaw dropped. How could it be? Tamarind Tiger was the name of his grandmother's sandwich shop in Cork. The name she had got from the Victorian cookbook she had inherited.

Chandran and Colin – Calicut, 29 June 1857

Chandran and Colin were at the Huzoor office. The telegraph room was at the back of the building, behind the canteen.

'Do you know how this works?' Chandran spoke in hushed tones. It was dark. The single oil lamp flickered in the corner. They would have to be quick.

'I've seen it once, on the very first day it was installed… '

Chandran looked at the man who had been the subject of so many of their jokes. He had also been the only white man in Calicut who joined them in their protest marches against the Company. Colin had changed. It was like a spark had been lit behind those green eyes. In the dark bowels of the Huzoor office, Chandran found Colin's drive invigorating.

'Peter won't be expecting a message. So we will have to add something that he recognises but does not raise suspicion amongst his colleagues.' Colin was working frantically.

'Are you sure of what you saw?' Chandran asked.

'I am certain. I saw the card in Chanakyan's hand—the rectangle of expensive vellum, with its bevelled border, and the engraving of the Greek Sea God, Poseidon, in the centre, with the trident and dolphin. I had seen it in Matheson's hand too, almost a month ago.'

'But could it have been something else?' Chandran asked.

'Matheson travelled to Calcutta as soon as he received the card. Chanakyan will travel to Calcutta too in a few days too. I overheard him making plans. The card is a missive. It has to be.'

'You think Poseidon is the name of their organisation? If that is true, then that is a breakthrough.'

'I have a strong hunch it is.'

'You think Peter will be able to capture Chanakyan and the rest of the Firm in Calcutta?'

'The Captain is our only hope.'

'Do you remember the day the Captain came to the house? He hid the shipping schedules inside the box of laddoos.' Chandran spoke, trying to lighten the atmosphere.

'I remember the laddoos. Wasn't it the only thing to eat that day because Carly had decided to take over the kitchen?'

'Yes, she served us plantain rice and hibiscus pacchadi.' Chandran laughed, remembering how they had all pretended to relish it and had then gone and thrown their lunch into the backyard afterwards.

'Why did the Captain call Carly Tamarind Tiger?' Colin asked, smiling. Chandran was only too happy to provide the story. He remembered the exchange as if it were only the day before.

'Cutie I must have puli for the chutney today.' Carly had commanded.

'But Carly, I have just grated a mountain of plantains for the chips. There is raw mango marinating in chilli for the pickle. Two pineapples have been chopped and are waiting for your attention. The ellisheri has everything in it but the kitchen sink.' Kutty Ettan had pleaded.

'Cutie, can you imagine the Ramayana without Hanuman?' Carly had negotiated.

Kutty Ettan submitted. 'Radha will help you. Radha, take Carly to the forest, please. She wants puli. One will do.'

'Kutty Ettan had a trick up his sleeve. Carly didn't know that he had asked Radha to fetch a tiger, not tamarind. Both words in Malayalam contain the same two syllables: 'pu' and 'li'. But their sounds are different. Radha, being the resident animal whisperer gave Carly an experience she would never forget. When the tiger turned up and brushed against Carly's skirt, she was so terrified.'

They laughed.

'Have you sent the message?' 'Yes.'

'Tamarind Tiger Chanakyan Poseidon HQ?' Chandran read the message aloud and looked at Colin. They both chuckled.

The telegraph never reached Captain Peter Charleston. Chanakyan never made it to Calcutta either. He was killed the next day, but the telegraph had made its way to Kannan a hundred and sixty-two years later.

4

Winds of Change

Sarah

Mother earth favoured animals when it came to confiding her deepest secrets and fears. She trusted her dearest with her insecurities. It explained why animals acted strangely days before an earthquake. Toads abandoned their ponds and snakes came out of hibernation.

Lucas had a bad knee. His doctor advocated physiotherapy but Lucas decided against it. His approach was more conventional. A walk had been the prescribed antidote to all manner of maladies through many Burtenshaw generations. To facilitate this walk, Westminster City Council cordoned off Little Italy every morning between 7:00 to 8:00 a.m. so that their most valuable citizen could exercise his bones.

Walking along the canal, Lucas pondered his conquests of the day. The Egyptian premier would be sworn in an hour's time. The premier had personally travelled to London to invite him. But Lucas considered his attendance of the investiture ceremony a superfluous engagement. He had already participated in the swearing-in ceremony in his mind when he had hatched his plan for Egypt two years ago.

Lucas had moved on to his next conquest. His focus was on his preparation for when the new prime minister of India would be sworn in. He would attend that ceremony. Deepika Pradeep would be the next prime minister of India. It was his dear friend Mohan's cherished dream for his niece. Lucas' participation in that event was without question; he would be a proxy for Mohan. There was also the small matter of the fireworks he had organised in memory of his friend.

His friend had died in an explosion in a petrol bunk. It was an accident. But the words the nun had said to him had echoed in his head:

'He is dead because of you.'

The nun visited him in his sleep every day. Sometimes, he saw the flames in her eyes and sometimes, he saw an iridescent blue network. He remembered the elation he felt thinking that Mohan had struck again. Just as Mohan had rid the journalist couple, Lucas had believed that Mohan had organised the kidnap and eventual murder of Edward Carringham and with that, the Burtenshaw vendetta would be complete.

But his euphoria had been short-lived. He received the news that Mohan K had been killed in a freak explosion at the petrol bunk. Since that day the nightmare had haunted him. The nun had spoken to him on each occasion. 'He is dead because of you'.

It had sown a seed of doubt that Lucas had indeed killed his friend; that the explosion in the petrol bunk had been ignited by a phone call he had made to Mohan K's mobile.

For the first time in his life, he had been scared. But he would not be beaten. He turned his fear into dogged determination.

And so he planned the fireworks. They would be unparalleled. They would set off simultaneously in the four metros of India. Deepika, his friend's protégé and niece, would assume the role of India's saviour and through her, Lucas would dominate. That would be sufficient payback for the nun's words and the death of his friend.

On his command, five hundred trucks carrying explosives would commence their journey to the four destinations: Chandni Chowk in Delhi, Stock exchange in Mumbai, the Howrah Bridge in Calcutta and Spencer's Plaza in Chennai. The fireworks would rage for ten days. Diwali would come early to India this year.

In his pre-occupation, Lucas did not notice the four who sat on a bench along the canal; a woman who sat at the edge of it. She put her hand on her daughter's shoulder and adjusted the callipers on her left leg. A young Indian man sat at the edge of the canal, his legs dangling in the water as he looked fondly at the girl on the bench. A man in Victorian breeches and a faded coat took out his flute and played a melody.

If Lucas had been more attentive, he would have wondered how birds, who were easily frightened off by human movement, allowed themselves to be coaxed onto the edge of the canal. Frogs and snakes from the canal swam ashore and joined in what looked like a procession of canal wildlife.

The wind picked up and the canal began to froth and bubble. Darkness suddenly descended. The boy continued to dangle his legs but this time, he turned towards Lucas. Lucas stopped in his tracks. He looked at the woman with the callipers and was seized by the memory of his uncle's portrait in his office falling without reason. A golden deer now sat nestled against her legs. Lucas jerked his head around, looking for cameras. Several film producers had courted the council for permission to shoot in Little Italy. But he did not see any tell-tale signs of a film set.

He returned his attention to the four on the bench. He studied them: three Caucasians and one Indian. He stared at the girl and saw marks on her dress. A cornflower blue dress with haphazard brown sprays. The pattern was beautiful, it was blood splattered by several bullets. The thought excited him. Lucas took out a small box from his pocket and sniffed the white powder.

The thought of guns, armaments of any size and shape gripped him with an unexplainable rush. His head thrummed with excitement. His eyes widened. His jaws tightened. His legs shook uncontrollably. It returned him to the fireworks he had planned for the subcontinent. It would be a spectacle that would be his finest yet. It was not a bad model for the rest of the world. He closed his eyes as though he were conducting the symphony. He imagined he was in India. He visualised the beasts roll in with their cargo of explosives into the expanse before him. He felt his body shudder with excitement. He took another sniff of the powder and felt a wave beneath his feet. He opened his eyes and was stunned with what lay before him. The trucks took the awesome forms of bears and rhinoceroses. The spray of gun fire showered him like the sparks in a furnace. The fireworks he had planned for India unfolded before him. He was ecstatic. His body swayed. A single monkey waved its tail as if it were a torch and everything around him was engulfed. He found himself surrounded by scorching brilliance. He felt the heat on his face. The orange specks danced on the pupils of his eyes. Flames touched everything. Smoke clouded his vision.

*T*he Earth mother was partial to these offspring. It was not only her pain that she confided but she also trusted them with her deepest joy.

It was not only in times of her pain that the snakes and toads came out. When justice was to be served, they came out in droves, along with their many, many friends.

Kozhikode

A nun in a *Mopilla* coffee shop could be considered a novelty but not in her case. She had been here so many times. She sat adjacent to a table where three youths sat. She caught snippets of their conversation while she pretended to pour over the menu. She was temporarily distracted by another customer, who lit his cigarette. Her attention was gripped by its flame and she was transported to the altar in the Infant Jesus Church with its hundred flickering candles.

She recollected how Edward had come to the church the first time. In February 1994, he had come to adopt the child. But the child had been adopted by another family. He had been devastated. Edward returned to the church twenty-four years later, just as she knew he would. But this time his life was in danger. While Edward waited for her at the church, she had met her friend at this very coffee shop.

She, in her white starched habit, and her friend, an Ayyappa devotee clad in black and numerous chains and charms, had caused quite the stir in the coffee shop. '*Chechi,* you called me? Urgent business you said. I came as soon as I got your message.'

'Thank you. When do you leave on your pilgrimage to Shabarimala?'

'This afternoon.'

'I need you to pick up my foreign friend from outside the Infant Jesus Church. Please don't be late.'

'Ok, *Chechi*. Is he a lost soul needing Lord Ayappan's blessing? Jesus not able to help?'

She laughed. 'He needs them both.'

She had made her way back to the church as fast as her legs could carry her. She saw the taxi parked outside, under the trees. She knew Lucas Burtenshaw waited inside it. Her skin tingled and the tattoo burned on her forearm.

Inside the church, Edward Stanley had been waiting for her. He was quietly observing the small congregation of nuns in prayer. She sat beside him and watched his eyes and the furrows in his forehead. He had a letter for the child which he gave to her before he left the church. It was many pages long. She promised she would post the letter. But the missive she actually sent to the child only had the words the child had needed to see.

'Find your scrapbook.'

Her friend had done as she had asked. With a couple of Ayyappa Swamy devotees, he had staged the kidnap of Edward Stanley Carringham. They bundled him into the bus and hurtled towards Shabarimala at speeds that would have done any Kerala bus driver proud. It had been witnessed by Lucas Burtenshaw, just as she had wanted. Lucas had believed that his associate Mohan had struck. Later that evening, Lucas had been informed that it was not Mohan's handiwork after all. Mohan had been killed in a car explosion in a petrol bunk earlier that day. A phone call, a petrol bunk, a thousand gallons of inflammable fuel and the motivation of one nun was all that was needed to carry out justice. She had visited Lucas many times after to remind him of his role in it.

Lucas Burtenshaw's scorched body had been found along a canal in Little Italy, London. Deepika Pradeep had withdrawn her candidacy a day before the election. Poseidon Holdings and its board of directors had been arrested for a terrorist plot to blow up key landmarks in four Indian cities. But what she was most grateful for, was the three descendants who had been brought together by her messages: an archaeologist, a journalist and an analyst.

She watched the three on the table adjacent to hers. Each was her own child. The girl for whom she had taken the oath and become a nun so she could keep watch over her in the Infant Jesus church; the Irish boy with the ginger curls, who had persevered relentlessly to get to the bottom of Edward's visit to the church and who had taken the photo of the girl's Bangalore address just as the nun had willed; the handsome journalist, to whom she had posted the extract from the registry and who was now sat here in the café.

The nun had taken the girl when she was a baby to the sacred resting place. Then Kalyani had been entranced by the fish in the water. Twenty-five years later, Kalyani returned to the subterranean chambers. She had found the secret protected deep in the womb of the earth.

She eavesdropped on their conversation one last time as the three planned their next move.

'When do we leave for London for the unveiling?' It was Kannan, the journalist who asked.

Kalyani didn't want to think of it. She only had the capacity to think of one life-changing event at a time. In an hour, they would meet with the Foreign Minister to discuss the arrangements for the transport and the security. The Director of ASI and the Major general would be there too. The last time she had seen the Director was when she had received her suspension orders.

Her fingers reached for the pocket tool in her pocket. It was her lucky charm. She had been right all along. The legacy of the ancient Indus Valley civilisation had survived. She had found it right here, buried under the noses of the residents of Kozhikode, under its most popular landmark—The Mananchira Tank.

She wanted to share her news with her best friend and confidante—the nun who had named her Baby Pongal. It was why she had come here with her new friends.

'You meet Sister Damu here every year?' Kannan asked Kalyani. She nodded and looked through the door impatiently.

'Is that her?'

A white car had pulled up outside. A thin English man got out.

The proprietor of the shop rushed out. Foreigners were good for business. This foreigner, however, was a loyal customer and a friend.

'Edward sir, Sister not with you today? There are three other people to meet her.'

The proprietor led Edward to where Kalyani, Liam and Kannan sat. 'Have you met?' The proprietor asked.

'No,' Edward said. But from the looks the four exchanged, they were certain they were connected inextricably.

The nun left the café. She looked back once more and then proceeded. The four had found each other. It was as she had intended. There was nothing more to do here. She had other commitments. He was waiting at the Thali temple for her—he and his faithful blue butterfly. It was the last day of *Karkidakam*. Sat outside on the steps of the Thali temple, he narrated the Uttara Kaanda.

'Sita's descent had marked the beginning of the end. Life was never going to be the same. A deep dark shadow had descended.'

Some of his audience, who were huddled outside the temple's threshold, wept as he recited the bittersweet end:

'Rama, followed by several thousand devotees, immersed himself in the Saraswathy River.'

It was the conclusion to the sacred Epic that the Seer of Meluhha had scribed thousands of years ago. She knew. She had been there all those years ago. It had all started with the vision. The Seer loved his homeland and his people. They had created paradise. Why then would its people cause its destruction? The vision had gripped his consciousness. He imposed the fourteen-year exile on himself to comprehend it. Surrounded by nature, being a guest at the Earth Goddess's ample dinner table with all her creatures, his first few years were blissful. The visions of animals and trees in distress seemed absurd. But gradually, he became acquainted with the small changes in the behaviour of flora, the altered moods of fauna and the effects on one another.

Then the visions came again thick and fast. In the quest for superiority and to emulate creation, his race had meddled with Earth's generous gifts. Long periods of selfish unchecked progress had created a mirage of outward perfection. But it had begun to corrode the insides. The Earth Goddess was being held captive, restrained and shackled by her own people. She had to be freed.

But the poison of unchecked human action had grown stronger. It became an untamed demon. When his people tried to rein it in, it became unwieldy. Out of bounds and out of their control, it propagated through the air and choked every plant and animal. There was only one way out. To get rid of the poison and to start again.

It was what had brought the Seer to her. 'I have a plan,' he said. 'The poison will be destroyed but so will all that have been tainted by it. It will burn and rage, an inferno will rise and reduce everything to dust. It will be at a great cost. But I need to be sure that the destruction will not be in vain and that the demon is well and truly destroyed. I will need your help.' he had said to her.

She knew the burden of the decision crushed him. Sleep deserted him. In deepest desperation and agony, he turned to writing. Twenty-four thousand verses of the epic poem—the Adi Kavya—was dedicated to his people, who didn't flinch from sacrifice. The selfless deeds of that great generation had been solidified into the hero of his story—Rama. The Earth Goddess they had wronged and wanted to rescue—Sita. The Seer of Meluhha had made their deeds immortal in his Epic.

The Seer and the people had asked her for help. How could she say no? She was under no illusion that her life would stretch forever. If it were to end, could this not be the most glorious and fitting way to do it? To embrace the most noble and supreme of God's creation and transport them to immortality. And so, on the appointed day she summoned the greatest force she could muster.

The explosion ripped through the streets, the houses, the dams and reservoirs and the fields. The evil poison burned. It spat and hissed all the time, reeling and turning like an angry tornado. The winds cajoled its angry currents and it hurtled towards her house. The Seer and his people were her guests. But she was ready for it. She wrapped around them and swirled. The demon railed against her banks angrily. It soon began to die. Its flames smouldered. She had sworn to wash away every trace of it and in doing so she had made her last journey through the Great Northern Plains.

But she had been given a gift. She could return when she pleased as Damayanthi the dancer or as sister Damu, the nun in the church. Her essence was captured in the Guardian's symbol of the sword and the vine that she wore on her arm as a tatoo. Look closer at the sword and you will see it isn't a sword but a river—the Saraswathy, rising in the mountain and flowing. Where she flows, life blooms.

5

River, Laughter, Moon & C

Carringham Gallery, London
(The Present)

'This has been an unusual auction. The combined British and Indian military presence has barricaded the entrance and exits to the Carringham gallery.'

Edward Carringham was getting into the swing of things. Not many got the chance to auction items for thirty million, sixty-one thousand, eight hundred and fifty-seven pounds.

'Sold,' he said not quite believing what had just happened. The scrapbook sat on the table oblivious to the commotion it had caused.

Kalyani, Kannan and Liam had been silent spectators. But when the scrapbook sold for that absurd price, the excitement was too much for Kalyani. She had shot off the bench and was followed promptly by Kannan and Liam. This was no time for adult composure. They escaped to the mezzanine that overlooked Edward's podium. They held hands and shifted on their two legs like kids – exhilleration yelling against the walls of their chests. They watched Edward Carringham carry on resolutely. It was the pocket tool's turn and it was under pressure.

'Do we have an opening bid on Item 2—a pocket tool from the mid-nineteenth century?'

The telephones rang at once. The staff in attendance quickly scribbled on their registers. The audience watched them with bated breath. The woman ran into the room again with her famous piece of paper and submitted it to Edward, the auctioneer.

'Sold.' Edward looked up at Kalyani, Kannan and Liam who were now standing on the mezzanine. Their eyes met and a feeling of overflowing gratitude surged through. As he enunciated the six digit price the numbers echoed. But then the surroundings became silent as though he had taken off into the stratosphere and his ear drums had collapsed under the pressure. In front of him the audience chattered but they were on mute. There were gestures of disbelief and gesticulations at the innocent pocket tool. But not a sound penetrated the invisible shield that had descended. He looked at his friends and from their faces he knew they felt the same. Then he heard a tinkling laugh. It was like someone trying to get the attention in a gathering of diners, like the tapping of a fork on a glass. From the expression on their faces, it was evident that Kalyani, Kannan and Liam had heard it too. The laughter sounded again. And then there were words garbled at first but only garbled because of the strong accent.

'*Aaji's pocket tool! That piece of junk?*'

'*Yes, Sound.*'

'*It is ridunculous ! Preposthmous!*'

A girl joined in. '*Did you do it Mr. C?* '

'*I won't take all the credit.*'

A school of uniformed military personnel had trooped in just then. The Auction had been concluded. Edward and his three friends ignored it. Their eyes desperately tried to sieve out the bustle and focus on the origin of conversation that they could hear.

Edward combed the sea of faces now scattered across the five floors of the lobby. The military had barricaded the entrance and exits and no one was allowed to leave.

There was more conversation. This time it was muffled as if the sound and its source had drifted. Edward stepped out of the hall that had been packed with six hundred people moments earlier. In the lobby he strained his ear. Kalyani, Kannan and Liam left the mezzanine above and joined him.

They reached the atrium. Here the core of the gallery had been scooped out. The Stele of Shu occupied the centre like a mythical bean stalk extending to the sky above only stopped on its voyage by a glass lotus dome. The sun shone through the glass. The jagged gold surface of the Stele cast mosaics of light on the opposite walls and the marble floor.

'He looks just like my brother...'

Edward jumped. The voice came from behind. He turned around. His heart thumped as he saw the shapes reflected in the wall.

'Mama, what did your brother call you?'

'Saaru.'

'What does it mean?'

'Means River.'

On the wall Edward saw the outlines of two people. Kalyani had seen it too. She traced the outline of the figure of the girl. Edward stared at the profile near the girl. It was that of a woman and the nose was big and beaked. That was a Carringham nose.

The reflections on the glass wall had grown. Thousands of small silver shapes surrounded now four definite forms. Kannan looked at the figures of the boy and girl holding hands in the reflection before him. He felt a current surge through his body as his hands grazed the hand of Kalyani. They were standing shoulder to shoulder together. Edward, Kalyani, Kannan and Liam stood rapt in attention, their attentions grasped by the unfolding reflections before them.

'They see us.'

'Look at Liam. He does have Carly's hair doesn't he and my chiselled chin of course.'

'Of course Mr. C,' a girl and boy chimed in.

'Aren't you two love birds in a good mood!'

They laughed. The laughter was hearty: the tinkling giggle of a girl, and the unrestrained laughter of young men. It was infectious. Edward, Kalyani, Kannan and Liam couldn't help smiling too.

Around them different levels of activity continued still enveloped by a sound shield. The soldiers trooped up and down as they escorted groups of philologists and historians to the Walls of Gold. Each examined sections of the inscription some making frantic notes and some consulting their tablets. A crowd of journalists had gathered in a side room. Press conferences were being held in an orderly manner. Intellectual experts were being courted like celebrities; All of their conclusions on a similar vein. The translation table on the Stele of Shu together with the etching on the Walls of Gold revealed the intimate account of the lives of the Meluhhans. It was a story of the greatest humans that ever lived; and had inexplicable similarities to the sacred Indian epic, the Ramayan.

'*It is moving.*' A sudden shout broke through the veil of silence.

The four spun around, their ears ringing as though they had landed on terra firma. The silence had been dispelled. The four tried to make sense of the flashing and sparks before them. The Stele of Shu had begun to spin. The radiance of the cylindrical tower was blinding. The floor beneath it shook, there was a quick rasp as the petals of the Lotus dome automatically opened and the tower seemed to ascend like it was growing. The tower uprooted from the ground. Carved into the base were four swans, their necks wrapped around the base. No sooner had the tower started spinning; the swans spread their intricate gold mesh wings.

There was a whirring as the thousands of gold feathers shaped automata dusted off the grime of centuries. Slowly and gradually, spreading further and further, the wings of the four birds followed a synchronised movement and lifted the tower. It hovered for a few minutes, occupying the well of light that had formed in the central atrium with the combined radiance of the sun and the moon.

Edward, Kalyani, Kannan and Liam turned around. The reflections on the wall had vanished.

'The Stele of Shu has ascended. The seated Goddess within the tower now stands. Her hand reaches out through the lotus dome of the building. We are getting aerial shots of a Vimana – the oldest flying machine.'

Outside, it seemed that nature was prepared for the premiere. The sky was a vision. It shone with alternating ribbons of silver and gold in a backdrop of salmon pink. The clouds had a luminescent quality, as if they were dusted with silver. The sun and moon were visible in the sky. Synchronised murmurrations of assorted birds across the skies complimented the spectacle that was unfolding below.

'We have breaking news from the salt marsh, fifty miles from Haryana, India. Can you bring our viewers up to speed?'

'It grows minute by minute and hour by hour. Hundreds have gathered: People on one side and elephants on the other.'

'Elephants?'

'The elephants have been streaming in for the last few hours. There are hundreds and thousands. The Indian army is trying to cordon the area. We aren't allowed any closer. The place is swarming with military trucks, tankers and helicopters.'

'For viewers just joining us, from 6:00 a.m. this morning, this stretch of salt marsh has been transformed by a freak series of events. Without warning, a rushing surge of water has bolted out of the fog, seething through a ravine. It has snaked through this terrain that has been bone dry for thousands of years. Incredibly, the river hasn't burst its banks. The ravine has contained it.'

'I was talking to a local. His camels graze in these marshes. These salt-encrusted plains have been here for centuries, unfit for cultivation. But in the span of the last twenty-four hours, this landscape has changed. Choppers have been scrambled to track the source. It has the buzz of a war zone; the air is heavy with anticipation.'

'Hold on; I have reports of a wild lioness.' 'A lioness?'

'Yes, a single lioness.'

'The elephants had retreated from the edge of the embankment. We thought they had gone to rest. Then there was a single cry from a swan. As though it were a cue, the elephants held their trunks up one by one, like a military salute. It was then that we saw her—the lone lioness, a majestic creature—walking slowly along the bank, escorted by the deer.'

'What is that orange glow behind you?'

'Those are people with lamps. Their presence has doubled since we spoke. There is a mood of awe and reverence. The army cordon hasn't discouraged them. If at all, it has brought more people to see this curious spectacle unfold.'

'The river is peaceful. You can see the reflection of the stars in her. It is a cloudless sky. Every star reproduced in the mirror like stillness of the river.'

'The people here say the ancient Saraswathy River has returned.'

THE END

Note to the Reader

Belief and Myth have made us innovators, creators, explorers, conquerors, believers. The power of an imagined reality has allowed us to achieve exponential progress. But for some time, we have become acquainted with the costs of that human cognitive superiority. What is damaged can be restored, what is pillaged can be nurtured and what is lost can be invited back. New realities need a new myth[1] and a new story to rally mankind.

I don't have delusions of coming up with that one life-altering myth. But I look back at what has been and wonder if it is possible that help is not far away. I ask if we can look at epics that have stood the test of time and revisit them with a fresh pair of lenses.

Every street has its own version of their beloved epic. The Ramayan started as an oral verse before it became a written script. It was chanted, handed from one generation to the next and in doing so, it transformed—a book of ancient wisdom embellished and coloured—and used as propaganda to suit changing times. But what if, at its core, it's a story of the wealth of human compassion and the power it wields. We were citizens of the planet before we were citizens of nations and followers of faith. Our ancient predecessors identified

---

1   Harari, Yuval N, Sapiens A History of Humankind (Harper, 2011)

with that Dharma—duty towards our planet and its beings. In today's advanced world, where compromise is old fashioned and courteousness outdated, we need a new story. United with flora and fauna, we are a force of good; disunited, we are the reason for destruction.

Author Biography

With a degree in Engineering and an MBA, Pavitra was all set to be another reliable widget of the great Indian production line. But this widget had a weakness. Fifteen years ago she was planted in British soil. An interest in history took root and she saw richness of India's past through borrowed lenses. She learnt that among the great civilisations, only the Indus Valley's script was still un-deciphered. Whilst Indians had made giant breakthroughs in every other sphere, their own ancient civilisation had stumped them.

Not one to shy away from a challenge, she decided to decipher the great Indus valley mystery using her copious imagination. She used the turbulent yet pivotal marriage between India and Britain in the 19th century as the moment of reckoning. Ever the optimist she offers hope. In her version the ancient legacy awaits in the shadows and is revealed with assistance from the supernatural.

River, Laughter, Moon & C is the result of her mind's machinations. It is a story of mortal acts and immortal consequence.

Lightning Source UK Ltd.
Milton Keynes UK
UKHW010624040320
359751UK00001B/106